The Theatre of
BHANU BHARTI

THE THEATRE OF BHANU BHARTI

A New Perspective

Diwan Singh Bajeli

NIYOGI BOOKS

Published by
NIYOGI BOOKS
D-78, Okhla Industrial Area, Phase-I
New Delhi-110 020, INDIA
Tel: 91-11-26816301, 49327000
Fax: 91-11-26810483, 26813830
email: niyogibooks@gmail.com
website: www.niyogibooksindia.com

Editor: Mohua Mitra/Niyogi Books
Design: Shashi Bhushan Prasad/Niyogi Books
Cover photo: S. Thyagarajan

ISBN: 978-93-81523-88-9
Publication: 2013

Printed at: Niyogi Offset Pvt. Ltd., New Delhi, India.

Dedicated to the Bheels of Udaipur, Rajasthan, who have kept alive their community theatre form Gavari for more than 4000 years

Contents

Foreword

Bhanu Bharti and I have been friends for about thirty years. Bhanu and I share two similar interests: literature and theatre. Our paths have often crossed in this regard. Bhanu is not only a playwright but also a director par excellence. I have seen him more as a director than as a playwright. This has heightened my respect and affection for him. He has been growing steadily from strength to strength with his innovative and creative productions. So far I have not been able to identify any other contemporary director who has shown such commitment to theatre. I have reasons for this statement.

Among contemporary directors, there are many who have turned towards the west and only a few who have turned eastwards for patterns and a framework for direction. A search for readymade patterns and frameworks has been on the rise in recent times. Bhanu has shown a dislike for such readymade patterns and has instead broken the boundaries and widened the scope of theatre experiments. Take his *Tughlaq* for example. The context of the play and the incidental details of the scenes were clearly and intensely portrayed along with the history of Tughlaq. The simultaneity of experience was outstanding. To be a part of the 5000-strong audience sitting spellbound and watching this new experiment was in itself a wonderful experience. Another production of equal stature was *Andha Yug*. I find Bhanu's extremely sensitive perception of globalisation, rising communalism, corrupt administration and the increasing fragmentation of society and culture quite remarkable. He has given a very sensitive portrayal of these contemporary elements and emerging social factors in his theatre. There is no doubt that he is emerging as a man with an extraordinary insight into the way the society is heading towards and the pitfalls that we may encounter in its course. His productions and plays are a testimony to this fact and his success is our pride.

An erudite publication of a director's success in theatre has not been done so far. This venture, I believe, is the first of its kind in the country. The book can justifiably lay claim to an international readership and the credit goes to Sri Bajeli. This venture will surely add to the stature of Indian theatre in the years to come. Sri Bajeli has at length discussed interesting details of theatre production and the creation of theatre text in his conversations with the director. He communicates the intricacies of theatrical elements and terms in a compact and precise manner while the lucidity and easy-flow of language make the book a pleasant, rewarding read. I am sure it will create history in theatre studies and my congratulations to Sri Bajeli for this effort.

Dr Chandrasekhar Kambar
Vice Chairman, Sahitya Akademi
former Chairman, National School of Drama Society

4 March 2013

Introduction

The eminence of Bhanu Bharti in the world of contemporary Indian theatre is reflected in his continuous search to explore and expand the frontiers of Indian theatre with deep roots in the soil of the country, revealing modern sensibilities. In this process his artistic vision keeps on widening in the context of socio-economic changes.

As a young man he was a witness to the great expectations of the Nehruvian era, which culminated in disillusionment. He continued his artistic discovery during the National Emergency (1975-1977) imposed by the former prime minister Indira Gandhi, using the allegorical language of theatre. Now in the era of globalisation and the dominance of multi-national corporations, he is keen enough to discover a new language for theatre to reflect the dilemma of humanity passing through a crisis; a crisis evident in the shape of commodification of culture.

The deep social concerns of his art, his trail-blazing innovations and the artistic complexities have always fascinated this writer who has had the privilege of watching most of his masterpieces in a variety of presentational styles. His staged his early productions with The National School of Drama and its repertory company attracted the attention of critics and a discerning audience. The staging of *Pashu Gayatri* at Natya Samaroh 1984, organised by Sangeet Natak Akademi at the Kamani auditorium was a major step towards the creation of a distinct Indian theatre idiom. This production catapulted him to national eminence. It was a significant experimental work which synthesised the elements of tribal art forms with modern theatrical techniques. Probably for the first time in the history of contemporary Indian theatre a play written by a modern writer was staged in Gavari style, a community theatre of the Bheels of the Mewar region of Rajasthan. The Bheel rituals were woven into the basic structure of the production to covey metaphorically that greed dehumanises man. The play was written by eminent theatre practitioner K.N. Panikkar.

Translated into Mewari by Deepak Joshi, the highlight of the production was that it was presented in the Gavari form with the original performers and for the first time outside their environment before an urban audience on a modern stage. Accompanied by Bhanu, I met some of these players in their village. They were happy that they performed Gavari outside their village and exuded a sense of achievement.

As a continuing search for an Indian theatre idiom, Bhanu has produced two more plays – *Kaal Katha* and *Amar Beej* – in Gavari style, giving a contemporary ring to the beliefs of Bheels, their rituals and legends. Undoubtedly, these productions have attracted the attention of Indian theatre practitioners and discussed at national seminars during the '80s. These were shown at most of the major Indian theatre festivals and there is still demand for *Pashu Gayatri*.

It is natural that these three productions should form part of the book and a special chapter on Gavari theatre form. Every year Gavari is celebrated in the month of August and continues for a month and a week. Watching Gavari with the entire village community is a unique experience. The play starts as soon as the sun rises and ends with sunset. The performers maintain celibacy and their diet remains strictly vegetarian. During the Gavari performance they stay at the temple and do not change their clothes all through the holy period of celebration. This is the theatre which could not be defined in terms of the total theatre of Brecht. It is the foundation on which the spiritual life of Bheels is built. This is the reason the form has been alive for about 4000 years. Bhanu Bharti has been able to capture the essence of this form in his experiments.

In an illustrious creative journey spanning about four decades. He was honoured by several leading cultural bodies including Sangeet Natak Akademi and Rajasthan Sahitya Akademi for his contribution towards the enrichment of contemporary Indian theatre and drama.

Apart from his in-depth study of rituals and art forms of the Bheels, he had studied traditional theatre of Japan in the University of Tokyo, especially Noh and Kabuki. He formed *Aaj Rangmandal* at Udaipur in 1984 to have continuous dialogue between the Bheel community and urban theatre practitioners on traditional and ritualistic forms of the Bheels and their creative use for modern theatrical art. He has also formed Aayam, a society for promotion of culture in Delhi which was registered in 1997.

As an eminent theatre personality he has occupied several posts including the director's at Shri Ram Centre for Art and Culture, that of the head of the drama department of Rajasthan university, Jaipur and also been the chairman of Rajasthan Sangeet Natak Akademi, at different stages of his career.

Bhanu is a total theatre artist—he is the director, playwright, designer and actor. He has excelled himself in all these aspects of theatrical art. He has directed about 100 plays. This study includes some his acclaimed masterpieces in the history of contemporary Indian theatre.

As a playwright of Hindi theatre he has invested his dramatic pieces with multiple layers. What we will discern are various stages of the growth of his artistry as a dramatist if we compare his early works with the most recent one *Tamasha Na Hua*. His plays reveal a distinctive sensibility and structure, which are marked by a departure from the traditional Hindi dramaturgy. He has great fascination for Asian art forms and literature. His play *Katha Kahi Ek Jale Ped Ne* is based on a Japanese tale. *Chandrama Singh Urf Chamku* is inspired by one of the greatest Chinese writers and father of new Chinese literature Lu Hsun's classic story *The True Story of Ah Q*.

Bhanu has elevated these plays to the level of allegory revealing the universal dilemma of humanity and the wounded soul of the oppressed. Again, inspired by Japanese dramic work his production of the Hindi version of *The Elephant* depicts the deeply painful and pathetic state of mind of the survivors of the atomic bomb explosion and the victims of the cadmium-polluted water supply. Physically deformed and socially boycotted as an outcast, these victims have their terrible world captured and depicted by the production very effectively. In most of Bhanu's productions we find a distinct sensibility that is different from the western theatre aesthetics—it could be described as an Asian one.

I have seen him rehearsing some of his recent productions. He is a hard task master and is a perfectionist. Everything in his concept of a play is precisely thought out. The music composer, light designer, set designer and costume designer are creative partners in his production process to evolve the right 'mise-en-scene', the expressive tones, rhythm and compositions. For Bhanu, theatre is the medium of the actor who is the live element in theatre through which the core intent of the play is conveyed and through which a lively rapport between the audience and the dramatis personae is established. So during rehearsals he gives special emphasis to the art of the actor, his accent, style of delivery and pauses to reveal the inner conflict of the character. Whenever he directs a play in Urdu, he invites an expert to correct the performers' accent though he has a fairly good Urdu accent.

After the completion of this project, he has directed two major contemporary plays—Bhanu's *Andha Yug* and *Tughlaq* by Girish Karnad. These two plays are considered classics in the history of contemporary Indian theatre and drama. E. Alkazi, the doyen of Indian theatre, had created waves when he directed *Andha Yug* for the repertory of the National School of Drama against the background of the old fort.

Earlier, Satyadev Dube directed it for Theatre Unit in 1962. Alkazi directed *Tughlaq* for the Repertory Company of National School of Drama which was staged at Kotla Ferozshah. It was a production that elevated the Indian theatre to a higher artistic pedestal. Bhanu undertook the adventurous creative journey to present *Andha Yug* in 2011 and *Tughlaq* in 2012. He presented these two plays against the backdrop of ruins of Kotla Ferozshah for the government of Delhi. Exploring the space of the theatre horizontally and vertically, he created magic with fresh interpretation. He dedicated it to his Guru, Alkazi who watched the production of *Andha Yug*. He was full of praise for the work of his talented student and declared that the production was world class. In both the productions he cast senior stage as well as Bollywood actors. Each production ran for a week and each day about a 1500-strong audience watched the show. His more recent play *Tamasha Na Hua* is a comment on national chauvinism and philosophical nihilism. The last chapter in this book is in question-answer format to present Bhanu's social and artistic concerns and his aesthetics and world vision.

I have tried to broadly give an objective view of the work of Bhanu, closely interviewing those who have worked with him. Commenting after going through the manuscript, Prof. of English and Sahitya Akademi award winning playwright Dr C.D. Sidhu wrote: "It is comprehensive: all aspects of Bhanu's theatre work have been detailed. It is authentic because it is largely based on the statements by the co-workers of Bhanu....It is a thoroughly researched work".

A life dedicated to theatre, Bhanu's art is multi-layered and has a vast canvas which perceives history and legends from the perspective of a modernist vision. This study will stimulate the interests of theatre scholars and critics to study Bhanu's work in greater depth and evaluate his contribution as an innovator in persistent search for a new idiom.

Fortunately for Indian theatre Bhanu continues to be in his best creative state of mind.

Diwan Singh Bajeli
11 February 2013

Poetic musings and political awakening

And since a perpetual equilibrium between man and the surrounding world cannot be expected to exist even in the most highly developed society, the idea suggests, too, that art was not merely necessary in the past but will always remain so.

Ernst Fischer (*The Necessity of Art*)

He was born on 16 July 1947. After thirty-one days of his birth into a Brahman family at Ajmer, Jawaharlal Nehru declared from the ramparts of Red Fort, 'Long years ago we made a tryst with destiny, and now the time comes when we shall redeem our pledge....At the stroke of the midnight hour, when the world sleeps, India will awake to life and freedom....'

This was the time British imperialism was forced to leave India. Breathing as a free nation in a free country, the people of India were bubbling with excitement, full of hope, dreaming of a new social and political order free from oppression. Gradually, the excitement started ebbing; feudal forces, which were allies of the British Raj, continued their exploitation. And underneath this seemingly jubilant surface, a movement to defeat feudalism was gaining momentum and being reflected in literature and art.

Bhanu Bharti grew up being educated and inspired by the anti-feudal political thought. His ideas were in tune with the progressive worldview of post-Independence India. As time passed this defiant young man grew into a theatre artist whose oeuvre is marked by innovation and a sincere quest for the creation of a truly indigenous theatre rooted in the soil and consciousness of the people, reflecting contemporary sensibility and social antagonism.

Bhanu's grandfather Pt Fateh Singh Maharishi was diwan of Bharatpur state. Known as Vakil, his main work was to liaison with British rulers. He had three wives. Bhanu's grandmother was the third one. After the demise of her husband she left Bharatpur to live alone with her son and bring him up. Bhanu's father Pt Hari Singh Maharishi cleared his Intermediate examination from Alwar. Being an owner of a *jageer*, he had the title of Sardar. His monthly income was ₹ 24, which was hardly sufficient to make both ends meet. So he took up a job at Mahalkhas Palace situated within Bharatpur's Lohagarh Fort, to substantiate his meagre income. In 1948 he was absorbed in the service of the state government as an office superintendent and transferred from Bharatpur to Jaipur.

Bhanu's mother Sumitra Maharishi was a housewife but she was fond of reading the works of Premchand, Sharat Chandra Chatterjee as well as the works of other contemporary fiction writers. She had a fascination for the poetic works of Mahadevi Verma. Bhanu imbibed his reading habit from his mother and by the time he was a young man, he had read a lot of books by prominent writers. This reading habit helped him in later years to seriously study world classics and political philosophy, which widened his intellectual horizon and developed his analytical faculties.

Bhanu recalls his mother's contribution to encourage him to have a sense of self-respect and to acquire a dignified place in society. He states the following episode when he was just in his early teens:

'As a young boy I was a fan of an immensely popular Rajasthani poet Megh Raj Mukul whose poem *Sainari* (Souvenir) – which stirred the Rajasthani masses with its heroic and patriotic fervour – highlighted the extreme sacrifice of newly-wed young Rajput women who inspired their husbands to fight their enemy in a bid to defend the country. I once heard him recite this heroic poem, took his autograph and went home jubilantly, rushing to show the autograph to my mother. Contrary to my expectations, she gave a cold response and told me, "Instead of getting others' autographs, strive to achieve something yourself so that people ask you for your autograph.' Ever since that episode I stopped collecting autographs.'"

After Independence the princely order existed only as a historical relic; the feudal forces however continued their oppression in one form or the other. Young Bhanu heard about the struggle of people for liberation from feudal oppression. Eulogising people's heroes like Shivaji, Rana Pratap and Bhagat Singh became an instrument to mobilise people. Bhanu was inspired to hear the poems rendered by the local poets to project the great deeds of patriotic heroes. He got the local children together to enact plays based on patriotic poems. Cots were used as stage and bedsheets as curtains. This improvised theatre, replete with poetic rendition fired the imagination of Bhanu. He was completely submerged in the noble ideals of patriotism. A self-styled freedom-fighter, he added a new title to his name and called himself Bhanu Bharti. His original family name was Brij Bhanu Maharishi. The act of discarding the family name 'Maharishi' was presumably influenced by Ram Manohar Lohia's socialistic ideas centred round a casteless society. He has been known as Bhanu Bharti ever since.

Among the most popular songs Bhanu and his childhood friends enacted was the song about Maharana Pratap's heroic fight against Emperor Akbar, The song runs like this:

Arye ghaasree roti hee
Jad van bilaawro le bhajyo
Naanho so Amroyo cheekh podyo
Rana rosato dukh jaagyo-
Hoon ladyo ghano, hoon sahyoghane
Mewari aan bachawan ne
Mein paach naheen raakhi ran mein
Wairaya ro khoon wah khan mein
Par aaj bilakhto dekhoo hoon
Jad raj kanwar ne roti ne
Mein chhatr dharam ne bhuloo hoon
Bhoolu hindwani choti ne

Translated to English prose, this would read: 'A wild cat snatched away the piece of bread made of grass. Little Amar Singh cried out as he was starving. Intense grief found expression in the aggrieved Rana's lamentations as he watched the misery of his starving little son living under extreme adversity. The confidence and heroic spirit of the Rana shaken and shattered, he lamented, "I fought many battles to save the honour of Mewar. I left no stone unturned and shed the blood of enemies mercilessly. But today when I see my little prince weeping as the wild cat snatched away his bread of grass, I feel inclined to discard my dharma as a Kshatriya and abandon the defence of the crown of Hind-Chittor"'.

At school too, Bhanu was enthusiastic to participate in plays. One of his favourite plays in which he took part was Upendra Nath Ashk's *Reshmi Tie.* Somehow his keen interest in theatre started slackening after a while; writing poems and short stories became his obsession. Bhanu would write for the children's supplement of *Rashtra Doot*, a leading newspaper of Rajasthan. Girls would often make fun of him and embarrass him by calling him '*kaviraj*'—a great poet.

Meanwhile, his elder brother Mohan Maharishi had started working in radio plays aired at the Jaipur radio station. At that time Om Shivpuri, Sudha Sharma, Nand Lal Sharma, Maya Asrani, Govardhan and Asrani were involved in radio plays at Jaipur station. Ganga Prasad was the producer of these radio plays and his brother Fakir Chandra Mathur was a producer of radio plays at AIR Delhi. Mohan Maharishi produced *Barat Aa Rahi Hai.* Bhanu was a keen listener of these plays.

He cleared his matriculation examination in 1960 at the age of sixteen. His brother Mohan had joined the National School of Drama, Delhi. It was Nehruvian era; there was talk of scientific temper and the need for science education to produce technicians and engineers for the economic reconstruction of the country to make the nation self-reliant. Bhanu's father wanted him to study science. He joined B.Sc (Agriculture) at Jobner Agricultural College, Jaipur.

'I was miserable there. It was a rural area. I was unable to adjust myself to the local ambience. I was short of attendence and left the college without having passed even first year. I was bitter and desperate to do something creative (which I) would enjoy … doing …' recalls Bhanu.

Once again he sought solace in writing poetry. He was welcome at poetic symposiums and given a hearing as a young poet. Soon after, he started working as an apprentice journalist in *Rashtra Doot*. Its editor encouraged him to write poems and feature articles. One of his popular poems of that period was this highly romantic piece:

> *'Kaun ho tum aansuon mein?*
> *Kaun shilpi aa ghusa hai prem*
> *ke toote sadan mein?*
> *Kaun ho tum aansuon mein?'*

(In English translation:

> 'Who are you in my tears?
> Who is the sculptor who has set foot
> On this shattered house of love?
> Who are you amidst the tears?')

It was the most romantic period in Bhanu's life when he thought he had finally found the real passion in his life—in writing poetry. A world of fantasy, romance and beauty was waiting to welcome him as a poet, he thought. Goodbye to journalism and to the study of science; poetry beckoned him and the idea filled him with ecstasy. However he received a sudden jolt while flying high in this land of poetic fervour and landed in the world of stark reality, which forced him to introspect and in the process acquire a new vision about life and society.

Bhanu was introduced to legendary freedom fighter Ganesh Lal Vyas by a friend. He was a poet, social reformer, a relentless fighter against feudalism and lived a simple life. In his modest home, doors were open to all that brought him closer to the common man. Complacent, Bhanu imagined that comrade Vyas would lavishly appreciate him as a poet but the reality was quite in the contrary.

'"You have a graceful body. Why don't you become a dancer?" commented comrade Vyas,' remembers Bhanu. 'I was flabbergasted,' he recounts, 'as I was hoping that he would talk about my poetry and encourage me to develop as a poet. Nevertheless, he used to take me to poetry symposiums where serious poetry would be eloquently presented as a critique of contemporary social dichotomy and class oppression. He had not even completed class IV in school but was an extremely well-read person and would compose poems with great felicity in English, Hindi as well as Rajasthani and was a regular contributor to the *Free Press Journal*, published from Mumbai. He led the masses to struggle for freedom from princely oppression in Jodhpur. He was put behind bars, tortured and forced to lie down on ice blocks which caused severe swelling in his legs. Undaunted by state oppression and economic hardship, Vyas continued to struggle and his conviction remained firm. A Brahman by caste, he had married the illegitimate daughter of a Thakur.'

Under his leadership Bhanu started reading books on Marxism-Leninism and by other great European writers. 'While talking about Marxism, comrade Vyas – who was affectionately called Ustad – never used jargon. His style of teaching Marxism was simple and forceful; his understanding of life was deep and his poetic conceptions were clear and free from obscurities,' says Bhanu. 'Once I went with him to a poetic gathering. The chief minister of Rajasthan at that time – Mohan Lal Sukhadia – was among the audience. Ustad recited his poem with these lines, addressing the chief minister:

> *'Ei dis padi na sukh ki chhain,*
> *Raj badalgyo*
> *Mhaane kaanee. . . .'*

(In English prosaic translation:

> 'Though the transfer of power has taken place but the masses continue to rot in misery and the ruling class grabbing money and power for themselves.')

'He was a real people's poet', Bhanu recalls. 'I was under his wings for two-and-a-half years. It was my true education. Ustad had affected my thoughts profoundly. Unfortunately, he died a tragic death caused by dog-bite.

'His death perturbed me emotionally and intellectually. I found myself alone, helpless and weak but his famous lines continued to inspire me:

> *'Le ke jamane se chalti hai kalam jinki*
> *Marte nahi kaza se ustad zindagi ke …'*

(In English translation the lines above would read:

> 'Writers who are inspired by the stark reality of life and society
> Remain steadfast in the face of adversity and misfortune.')

Bhanu started writing serious articles on the contemporary political scene, besides once again composing progressive poems and short stories which were being published in leading newspapers and magazines. Not an armchair intellectual, he got himself involved in the student politics of the state. This was the period of students' radical movements all over the world. Bhanu was deeply influenced by the students' movement in France which was aimed at replacing the bourgeois exploitative system with a new and just social order in alliance with the working class. He threw himself heart and soul into the student movement, joining them in the burning of certificates awarded by the university in public and protesting violently against unemployment and exploitation of the working class.

'This was the most exiting period of my life when I experienced the power of fraternity in the student community,' remembers Bhanu. 'This was during the mid-1960s. Apart from reading on Marxism, I began to read the works of Jean Paul Sartre, Albert Camus and Franz Kafka. Unfortunately, students' protests, which had been sweeping through most countries, gradually started to fizzle out', says Bhanu. He wrote in a reflective mood, 'Most student leaders proved to be opportunistic and had compromised with their ideology and I became disillusioned with the prevailing state of the student protests.'

Bhanu was once again at the crossroads. He was facing an intellectual and emotional crisis. Meanwhile, his elder brother Mohan Maharishi had graduated from the National School of Drama (NSD), New Delhi—India's premier institute for theatre training. He went to Germany and joined Berliner Ensemble to study Bertolt Brecht's theatre, its technique, aesthetics and philosophy. 'I remained in Germany to learn Brecht's methodology as was being followed by Berliner Ensemble,' Maharishi had once said during an interview. 'Brecht was no more. His widow Helene Weigel was the director. I was studying under her guidance. I watched the actress in the plays *Mother* and *Mother Courage*. Her methodology was remarkable for detailed and minute preparation of all aspects of Brechtian technique. She was passionately keeping alive her husband's epoch-making theatrical art and was honoured with the highest award in the field of creative art by the German Democratic Republic. I am happy that she took personal interest in teaching me the Brechtian technique', said Maharishi during the same interview.

After having trained at NSD under E. Alkazi – the doyen of Indian theatre – Maharishi returned to his hometown Jaipur with new ideas and techniques from Helene Weigel (Berliner Ensemble, Germany). He founded Sanket, a theatre group, promising to herald a movement of art theatre in Jaipur.

'During those days comedies were popular on the Jaipur stage. Pinchoo Kapoor was a leading theatre practitioner of this genre. Ranbir Singh, a playwright, was campaigning for a meaningful theatre movement. Radio plays were more popular and radio actors – who often appeared on the stage – commanded respect from the audience. During those days audiences considered the medium of radio and stage to be somewhat similar. It took considerable time for people to understand that the two are different mediums,' said Mohan Maharishi.

Maharishis's entry into the Jaipur theatre scene was a great event. He directed several outstanding productions. 'As a student of Alkazi I was trained that casting should be done strictly on the basis of merit. I was casting for *Bhoomija*, the Hindi version of Mama Warerka's Marathi play *Bhoomi Kanya Sita*. I decided to cast Bhanu in the role of Lav. He was then slim, smart, bright and passionately involved in the student movement, with a following among the student community. He gave a wonderful performance. It occurred to me that he was cut out for a great career in theatre. As an actor he was simply amazing.'

Maharishi was very strict about punctuality at rehearsals. It was a new experience for theatre actors of Jaipur altogether and their first opportunity to work with a theatre director of Maharishi's calibre who had a deep insight into complex theatre production techniques and a profound knowledge of contemporary aesthetics. Maharishi was trying hard to instill into theatre workers of Jaipur a sense of discipline and commitment. So far, they had been doing a kind of theatre that hardly matched the concept of 'theatre' as he understood.

Maharishi narrated one of the incidents that occurred while imposing discipline on Bharti. 'One day Bhanu came one hour late at the rehearsal. I became furious and shouted at him. It was a new experience for him, who as a student leader was … admired and even feared. He remained silent for a while and joined (the) rehearsal process without uttering a word but the rebel in him continued to manifest itself in many ways for several weeks. He stopped talking (to) me. However as an actor he remained devoted to his work.'

Impressed with Bhanu – who had proved himself and delivered riveting performances – brother Maharishi cast him in several plays like *Mother* and *Shuturmurg (Ostrich)*. Originally written by Gyandev Agnihotri of Kanpur, the script of the play *Shuturmurg* was rewritten by Maharishi and Dr Bharat Ratna Bhargava – a playwright and theatre scholar – in which Bhanu was cast in the role of Bhashan Mantri. The year was 1966 and this was a pungently satirical piece of theatre commenting on the corrupt and inefficient political class. This particular production would be remembered in the history of theatre movement in Jaipur as a milestone as far as political satire was concerned. 'It received wide publicity,' Maharishi recalls. 'From Delhi came Mohan Rakesh and Habib Tanvir to (watch) it. The then education minister of Rajasthan – Barkatullah Khan – was invited to attend the premier. As the (play) began to unfold, the satire became (increasingly) bitter, establishing direct rapport with the audience ... pent-up frustration, anguish and protest against the anti-people policies of the government (were) directed at the education minister who was forced to leave the auditorium as the audience started shouting at him. An angry and red-faced minister rushed to the chief minister who was hosting a dinner party. The education minister demanded my arrest for provoking people to protest violently against a democratic government. Later, our journalist friend who was invited to the dinner told me that their chief minister pacified Khan.

'The group was invited to perform in Delhi where it was a runaway success. Alkazi invited us to the dinner organised on the terrace of his flat. Among others who were present at the dinner (were) playwright Gyandev, Mohan Rakesh, Uma Anand, Bharat Ratna Bhargava and N.C. Jain. Gyandev was furious (with us) for changing his original script. However, his ... feelings were assuaged by Mohan Rakesh. Bhanu – who had given an excellent performance – was also present. A bit bewildered, he was discovering the world of eminent ... artists of contemporary Indian theatre.'

Introduced to the magical world of theatre art, which could prove to be a weapon in his socialist struggle, Bhanu was on friendly terms with his elder brother; they would discuss art, culture and literature on equal terms like comrades. Commenting on the theatre scene of Jaipur in those days, Bhanu says, 'Mohanji had brought about a revolutionary change (in) the very concept of theatrical art. It was the time when people had harmonious relationships and social life was peaceful. Politicians in power were accessible; they would come and interact with people. Mohanji inspired a host of talented artists like Ila Pandey, Rama Pandey, Meenakshi Thakur, Vijay Bakaya and Vasudev Singh and was able to build up discerning theatre audiences but times changed; Mohanji joined Delhi Doordarshan as producer in 1970. Gyan Kaushik joined BBC, Vinod Sharma and Pinchoo Kapoor went to Bollywood.'

Though critically acclaimed by the audience as an actor, Bhanu did not take theatre seriously. He was disenchanted with the student politics of his state. Young, proud, sensitive and restless; he wanted to do something different, exciting and meaningful in life. Unable to realise those dreams in Jaipur, he was desperate to leave his hometown.

He had a chance meeting with Alkazi in Delhi who knew him already as the younger brother of Mohan Maharishi and as a talented stage actor. Alkazi asked him, 'Would you like to join the National School of Drama?'

'No, I don't want to make theatre my career', replied Bhanu rather curtly, drawing an end to the episode quickly.

Life at The National School of Drama: a bitter-sweet experience

I try to say how the world appears to me as sincerely as possible ... I try to be the objective witness of my subjectivity. When writing for the theatre I am only concerned with personifying, in a tragic and, at the same time, comic sense. That shouldn't prove a difficult problem ... trying to be avant-garde before writing, not wanting to be, or refusing or choosing which kind of avant-garde it is to be, is, for someone creative, going about things the wrong way.

Eugène Ionesco

This angry and ambitious young man from Jaipur landed in the capital city of India and got admission to The National School of Drama in 1970. It was altogether a different world for Bhanu Bharti. In Jaipur he was a student leader, respected and surrounded by his followers, enjoying freedom and somewhat his own master. Suddenly, he found himself in an atmosphere of elitist culture and felt almost like a fish out of water. But his sense of defiance did not betray him and found manifestation on the day of the admission test itself. 'There were two sets of papers for admission seekers. When I saw this I went to Alkazi to ask him why there were two sets of question papers and this discrimination,' Bhanu remembers.

'He said that those like Naseeruddin Shah and I who have a theatre background should be given preference. Obviously, Alkazi did not like being questioned by an applicant. But for me coming from Jaipur, barging into the vice-chancellor's office was just a simple means of protest. NSD director Alkazi was a stern disciplinarian and my behaviour was unpardonable. (However) my brother Mohan Maharishi, who had passed from NSD with flying colours, was Alkazi's favourite student (and) my act of unwarranted defiance was not taken seriously.'

Initially, Alkazi considered Bhanu a book-worm. In the first year he obtained seventh position in the class and in the second year he was placed in the seventeenth position. The third year was marked by violence with a classmate, bitterness and finally the celebration of achievement at the close of the session and a sense of *joie de vivre*. What he confronted in the third year was something unusual. He recounts his experience as follows.

'It all happened in the course of a rehearsal of *Razia Sultan*. Naseeruddin Shah was a pampered student of Alkazi. He was physically strong and tried to bully me. I refused to surrender and retaliated, resulting in a physical fight. When this matter was brought to the notice of Alkazi, he ignored my complaint. On the contrary, he shielded him. I was deeply hurt, bitter and found myself completely isolated. A stage came (when) I planned to quit school. My sister-in-law Anjala Maharishi was warden of the school hostel at that time. When my brother came to know about this violent incident, he was anguished at the partisan attitude of Alkazi. My brother met him.'

According to Mohan Maharishi who met Alkazi to resolve the matter, 'Bhanu was physically not strong. He was dragged and started bleeding as a result of a violent clash between him and Naseer. I requested Alkazi to be fair in the case. Bhanu has an independent nature; he does not want interference in his affairs but when this injustice was brought to my notice, I could not resist myself.

'In my discussion with Alkazi for whom I have great respect it appeared to me that he was defending Naseer, with little sympathy for Bhanu. I decided to stand by my brother even if he had to sacrifice his career in defence of his human rights.'

However, the matter was solved but Bhanu and Naseer were not on speaking terms—a kind of hidden hostility lingered between them.

Bhanu's life at the school continued as usual; he was pursuing his studies diligently. Three students were selected for the course of direction. These were Asha Kasbekar, Rajan Sabharwal and Bhanu.

Soon it was time for presenting the directorial diploma production. Bhanu once again had an argument with Alkazi who wanted him to produce a Hindi play as he came from a Hindi-speaking region. Bhanu was adamant that he would direct Eugène Ionesco's *The Lesson* (1951). It is an important work in the Theatre of the Absurd. Its technique and philosophy were too complex to convey the essence of the play clearly—the inadequacy of the language of communication, the feeling of absurdity and the grotesqueness that awaits human fate. Once again there was tension in the class. Bhanu recounts one incident. 'In an oblique reference to my choice of presenting an absurd play, Alkazi said, "People do not walk on their heads in Absurd theatre." I commented promptly, "Thank you, Mr Alkazi, I indeed thought that people walked on their heads in Absurd theatre."

'I was feeling insulted and humiliated and was ready to quit the school. However, I was allowed to present *The Lesson*. In fact, I had great fascination for Samuel Beckett and wanted to stage his *Waiting for Godot* but it had already been done by another student. Now my first task was to do casting. There are three characters in the play: Professor, Maid and Student. I selected Naseer to act as the professor. Everybody was taken aback because I was not on speaking terms with him. Jyoti and Jayashri were selected to play the student and the maid respectively.

'I had accepted the challenge to direct an absurd play. I studied existential philosophy, writers of the Theatre of the Absurd like Samuel Beckett, Eugène Ionesco and Arthur Adamov who highlighted the absurdity of human existence and the metaphysical anguish of humanity.

'The budget allocation for the production was ₹ 250 only. After working hard for twenty-five days came the day of presentation. I had designed a box-set with two doors; one was kept open and the other one was bolted. There was no use of music; and for sound effects, the sound of footsteps and thumping on the desk were used. There were (also) long silences.

'Everything was in place. As the play began, it was discovered that both doors were bolted. I (went) simply blank and thought it (would turn out) to be a disaster. Somehow Jayashri managed to open the door. The play went on smoothly as conceived. I was enraged by the bolted doors and thought that somebody had tried to sabotage my production, planning to ruin my production and my career. Luckily Alok Mardana finally mentioned that it was he who had bolted both the doors by mistake. I felt greatly relieved.

'The production was a grand success. The members of cast and crew were in the room. Naseer and I looked at each other's faces and had a hearty laugh; we embraced each other, all our past quarrels and animosity disappeared in that moment of ecstasy. Ever since we became very close friends.

'As we were embracing each other, Alkazi entered the room and said, "As soon as you complete your love scene come for viva."'

An emboldened Bhanu was ready to face the examiners. The following were a few of the questions he was asked:

'Why were the shoes not appropriate?'

'There was no budget,' he replied.

'Why you have not used music?'

'The silences and offstage sounds were themselves music.' Alkazi smiled at the way he answered questions.

'Can you adapt it,' he asked Bhanu.

'No, you cannot adapt poetry. The play is a dramatic poem,' came Bhanu's prompt reply.

❧

It was December 1972. This was the year that marked the watershed in Bhanu's life. The tension, bitterness and uncertainty were finally over in his life at NSD.

This young man from Jaipur with dreams, who found himself an alien in the elitist atmosphere of NSD, surprised everyone by standing first in the class. He was adjudged the best director and the best all-round student. He was pleased with himself when the classroom production of *The Lesson* had public shows, keeping in view the artistic excellence of his direction.

A French lady also came to watch this production (she had seen the play in Paris) and said that Bhanu's production of *The Lesson* was much better. This was in itself a great tribute to Bhanu's directorial art.

Reflecting on his life at NSD, his troubles and confrontations with the authorities, Bhanu said that NSD has left an indelible impact on his lifestyle and career. He was leading a life of anarchy in Jaipur; sometimes he would remain awake all through the night, busy in discussions with students and at times he would not even eat properly. At NSD he had to follow strict discipline to chalk out his working plan.

'I have great respect for Alkazi', reflects Bhanu. 'His method of teaching was superb; he would make the basics of theatrical art very clear, which provided me with the key to understand the theatre of any country, her [*sic*] past and present. My classmates were highly talented. We were a class of eighteen students and out of these six were girls who used to wear saris in those days. The quality of food served at the hostel was poor. For fun we would often become freeloaders in hotels [*sic*]. There was a lot of work to do and a lot to read and discuss. It was a qualitatively different life from that in Jaipur—a life more focused on work.'

After obtaining his degree from NSD, Bhanu joined its Repertory Company for a year. His directorial art was displayed in two plays—*The Lesson* and *Ras-Gandharva,* which merit special mention.

On the basis of the success of *The Lesson*, there was a demand that Bhanu should direct this play for the Repertory. What was remarkable about this new version was the fact that far from being a carbon copy of his class production, it revealed Bhanu's fertile imagination, the use of a variety of theatrical techniques and his perceptive mind interpreting the Theatre of the Absurd in different ways.

In the school production he had used a box-set while in the Repertory production the play unfolds on the bare stage. In the previous production he treated the character of the maid as a positive force counter-pointed by an evil force represented by the professor. But later on he realised that the maid held the string and the professor was a mere puppet in her hands.

As director he was able to penetrate deep from a comic surface into the reality of human condition and the chain of awareness of the impending death of man and its subsequent fallout remains unbroken; the maid reveals the philosophy of the absurd when she says, 'Arithmetic leads to philosophy and philosophy leads to crime.' As the excited and angry professor stabs his student, the maid announces that this is his fourth murder in one day and ushers in a new student. This production was widely acclaimed by the audience and it had several weekend shows at the Studio Theatre.

Om Puri as Professor, Jyoti Deshpande as Student and Uttara Baokar as Maid gave outstanding performances.

Another of Bhanu's groundbreaking productions for the Repertory was *Ras-Gandharva* (1974) by Mani Madhukar, a poet and Hindi playwright who sought to break away from western moulds and follow indigenous forms. Structurally inchoate, the play is a unique combination of Indian mythology and traditional elements with the western concept of the Theatre of the Absurd. Politically, it comments on the failure of the Nehruvian concept of an egalitarian society which he described as a socialistic pattern. The play signals the danger of the emergence of a dictatorial polity in which the dissenting voices were silenced by a totalitarian state.

The action moves in a rather illogical manner from the past to the present and vice-versa, from fantasy to reality. The comic element ranges from farce to burlesque, irony and satire. As told by Bhanu, Alkazi described the play as a chain of jokes.

As a keen observer of contemporary Indian politics, Bhanu discovered in *Ras-Gandharva* the images of disillusionment of the post-Nehruvian era. He describes in the following lines his method of conceptualising the production:

'After several readings of *Ras-Gandharva* I rewrote the second part to give some kind of coherence to the script. Unwanted jokes were edited, the chorus was deleted and the names of characters were changed.

'I designed the production. The stage was almost bare with tree stems. The costumes were also designed by me. I used puppets to incorporate the element of the Theatre of the Absurd. The mythological characters were treated in the form of fantasy and the contemporary ones were placed in a realistic mode.

'As far as the political connotation of the play is concerned I tried to invest the production with the idea that a state apparatus – for that matter any political system – reflects clashes of egos and eccentricity of a ruling class which leads to social and political anarchy with its concomitant dangers of dehumanisation.

'Members of the cast consisted of great actors like Manohar Singh, Uttara Baokar, Balraj Pandit, Rajan Sabharwal and Surekha Sikri. Jyoti Deshpande and I played the role of Nirdeshak. As the beloved of the court poet, Uttara acted in the style of the puppet, her movements were manipulated by a puppeteer using his *pipadi*, a typical musical instrument used in traditional puppet plays. It was a great experience to watch her. Manohar Singh played three roles—a physically challenged police man, Lekhak and Afsar. He had acted in great roles in plays like *Tughlaq* and *Othello*. Here in this comic role of the policeman he was eminently comic, evoking audience laughter. It gave me great satisfaction when in one of his TV interviews he talked about his role of the policeman in my production of *Ras-Gandharva*, describing it as a memorable role for a comic actor in his illustrious acting career.

'The production was staged at the open-air theatre Rabindra Bhavan and became immensely popular. Apart from regular theatre goers, there was a steady stream of common (people) to watch a comedy they thought (was) highly diverting.'

Bhanu's tenure of one year came to an end. This period with NSD Repertory was fruitful for him and his art began to be acknowledged by serious art theatre circles. But he remained dissatisfied with his work; he wanted to explore new innovations in theatrical art, discover new playwrights and find greater artistic freedom.

As soon as he came out of the Repertory, he embarked on a new creative journey, experimenting with new theatrical forms, analysing thematic elements of plays in the context of changing social reality. Delhi, Jaipur and Lucknow became his centres of activity.

As he was struggling to comprehend the existential concept of 'Being and Nothingness' and the Theatre of the Absurd's basic concerns 'to express its sense of the senselessness of the human condition', he found Bhuwaneshwar Prasad's *Tambe Ke Kire*. Describing it as an excellent piece of the Theatre of the Absurd by an Indian playwright, he produced it in 1974. In the opinion of a discerning audience it was a hallmark of excellence. A leading Hindi magazine of that time carried a special feature on the production with the photographs of the most vital scenes of the production on its cover page. A detailed critique of the play followed later.

Bhanu's journey into the most exciting, rewarding and ever-expanding horizons of theatrical art has many milestones which are to be discussed in the forthcoming chapters.

In quest of creative freedom

Hamlet: Denmark's a prison.

Rosencrantz: Then is the world one.

Hamlet: A goodly one, in which there are many confines, wards and dungeons, Denmark being one o 'the' worst.

William Shakespeare *(Hamlet, Act II Scene II)*

What I have in mind is not a forced topicality, a Hamlet that would be set in a cellar of young existentialists. Hamlet has been performed, for that matter, in evening dress and in circus tights; in medieval armour and in Renaissance costume. Costumes do not matter. What matters is that through Shakespeare text we ought to get at our modern experience, anxiety and sensibility.

Jan Kott (*Shakespeare Our Contemporary)*

His one-year stint at the NSD Repertory Company established Bhanu Bharti as a perceptive, imaginative and innovative stage director, who was determined to go beyond his alma mater (NSD) as far as creativity was concerned and eager to search new ways to create a theatre with a new perspective. 'During those days artists for the Repertory were engaged for a year with a possible renewal for another year,' Bhanu recalls. 'I told Alkazi I would leave Repertory after a year. Those days Alkazi was struggling to make NSD independent of Sangeet Natak Akademi. When my tenure came to an end, N.C. Jain was officiating director because Alkazi was on leave … If I wanted I could have got my contract renewed. I wanted freedom to create a theatre that is close to my vision of art and society. At the Repertory I felt the atmosphere stifling where things were followed in a routine manner. So I decided to come out and form my own platform with the help of friends like Rati Bartholomew, Neelam Mansingh Chowdhry and Raj Babbar. The name of the group was Sub Rang.'

Most of the members of Sub Rang Theatre Group were NSD graduates, full of new ideas and enthusiasm. Bhanu decided to direct Shakespeare's *Hamlet*, an ambitious and challenging task. The group had little money and was not registered. The year was 1974. Bhanu gave a graphic account of the ordeal he and his team of young artists went through while producing *Hamlet*:

'We booked AIFACS auditorium for the show. Since the group was not registered we had to go from pillar to post to get entertainment tax exempted. With the help of some journalist friends we met the then chief minister Radha Raman for this but it was all in vain. We had no money to pay the rental charges of the auditorium.

'However, the rehearsals went on in the foyer of Shri Ram Centre with nominal payment. Tarseem Lal was assigned to make sets. There were various levels and pillars. Wooden material priced at ₹ 3500 was obtained on deferred payment. Saba Zaidi was asked to design costumes but we had no money to buy material (and) had no place to stay. Ravindra Bhavan's cycle stand served as our night shelter. During the day we would roll up our beddings and leave them at the stand. As far as food was concerned, Lalaji at Refugee Market near Bengali Market was kind enough to allow all of us to eat at his hotel and pay him later. One night it rained heavily and at the cycle stand we could not sleep and remained awake [*sic*] the whole night with our beddings and clothes all wet. Only a few days were left for the presentation. We invited Alkazi to see our rehearsals; he (approved of) the way (the) rehearsals were being conducted … (as well as) the casting....However, just before the day of the show Neelam Mansingh Chowdhry managed to collect ₹ 10,000. This was a great achievement keeping in view our limited resources and contacts. This enabled us to stage the play in which we had put our heart and soul, (overcoming) formidable obstacles.'

Bhanu had not much experience in staging Shakespeare. He supervised the lighting in *Othello*—directed by Alkazi. 'It was one of the three bad productions by Alkazi, the other two being *Razia Sultan* by Balwant Gargi and Laxmi Narayan Lal's *Surya Mukhi*', he recalls. What then, motivated him to do *Hamlet*?

'I was inspired by Jan Kott's *Shakespeare our Contemporary*. I was also reading the reviews of Peter Brook's productions of Shakespeare's plays in *The Drama Review* (TDR)—a pre-reviewed academic journal focusing on performances in their social, economic, aesthetic and political contexts. I read *Hamlet* several times and found the striking relevance of this classic written about 400 years ago to our current situation. I was overwhelmed with the modern analysis of *Hamlet* by Kott. But my interpretation of the play goes beyond what Kott conceived.

'I was not convinced with the end of the original; it was (much) too idealistic (for my liking). The absurdity of the real world was more cruel and grotesque. Evil represented by King Claudius could not be destroyed as easily as depicted in the original. The other factor that intrigued me most was that the friendship of Hamlet and Horatio was far from idealistic. In a kind of world we are living, true friendship is impossible. To me Horatio betrayed Hamlet and King Claudius did not die. Both Horatio and Claudius move together in their unholy, unethical and unashamedly opportunistic alliance to greet the new king Fortinbras. Before breathing his last, Hamlet watches this betrayal by a person whom he loved and trusted from the bottom of his heart. Of course this ending was not received well by critics and a section of audience. This issue became the subject of debate in the theatre world of the capital those days.'

Bhanu explains in detail the socio-political aspects of *Hamlet* that make it a contemporary play. 'Something is rotten in the state of Denmark' and 'Denmark's a prison' are the significant dialogues that reflect the anxieties of contemporary Indian youth. 'Young people of my generation were passing through a transition in the 1960s and 1970s. The youth were disillusioned with the failure of Nehruvian high-sounding political and economic socialistic goals. The Gandhi-Nehru legacy was forgotten. Rank opportunism and sycophancy took centre stage. It was the period of Indira Gandhi [*sic*]. The dilemma of (the) idealistic youth of that period appeared to be (the same as) that of Hamlet who found Denmark rotten. That was the reason I decided to do *Hamlet*.'

'Not only India but the entire world was also passing through a crisis', Bhanu continues to explain the diverse factors in play during those turbulent times. 'The victory of communism in Russia and formation of the Soviet Union and the Socialist Republic of China promised the dawn of a new civilisation based on equality of opportunity, freedom from political and economic oppression and an end to the war of aggression. But what happened in Poland in 1956 was a shock to all those who believed in Marxism. There were massive anti-government and anti-soviet demonstrations. Soviet tanks moved into Poland to suppress the mass movement for higher wages and trade union rights. At home the Communist Party of India was marred by sharp ideological differences which resulted in the split in 1964. The new formation was called Communist Party of India (Marxist). All these developments left progressive youths of my generation confused, lost and bewildered. The international Communist movement was ideologically divided. The polemics between the CPSU and (the) Chinese Communist Party acquired irreconcilable dimensions. The idealism of Indian youth was crushed with the brutal suppression of (the) Naxalbari movement in the early 1970s. More than 10,000 men and women gave their lives and many more were imprisoned. It was most inhuman. As a theatre artist I found the reflection of my generation in *Hamlet* and I called it *A Hamlet*.'

In producing *Hamlet*, Bhanu had many problems regarding both organisation and finance. There were three Hindi translations of the play available—one was by Harivansh Rai Bachchan, another by Range Raghav and the third one was by Amrit Rai. He chose the third one which was in prose but with his sensitive treatment of various expressive means on theatre and the rhythmic flow of acting style Bhanu created a poetic language on the stage.

Bhanu's Hamlet does not feign madness. 'I think we all suffer from temporary madness,' Bhanu remarks. 'It (is) acknowledged by psychiatrists that when we are unable to cope with acute anxiety and find ourselves in a state of mental delirium, we lapse into a state of temporary madness. (The same) is true of Hamlet. Samuel Beckett in *Waiting for Godot* puts (it) this way—"We are all born mad and some remain so."'

❧

Bhanu's controversial ending of *Hamlet* had raised many eyebrows. Having read Bertolt Brecht's *Little Organum for the Theatre* where Brecht wrote, 'The theatre should always be mindful of the need of its time. Let us take, as an example, the old play of *Hamlet* ... ', Bhanu found the contemporary Indian socio-political scenario more barbaric, bloody and gloomy (than the situation in *Hamlet)* and hence he changed the interpretation of the character of Horatio. A dying Hamlet, says to Horatio:

'As thou'rt a man,
Give me the cup: let go; by heaven, I'll have't.
O good, Horatio, what a wounded name,
Things standing thus unknown, shall live behind me!
If thou didst ever hold me in thy heart
Absent thee from felicity awhile,
And in this harsh world draw thy breath in pain,
To tell my story.'
As Hamlet dies, Horatio says:
'Now cracks a noble heart. Good night sweet prince:
And flights of angels sing thee to thy rest!
[March within.]
Why does the drum come hither?'

In brief, Horatio is a most faithful friend of Hamlet and he remains true to him throughout his life. But in Bhanu's production he betrays

Hamlet by leaving a dying Hamlet alone and accompanying Claudius to welcome the new king, Fortinbras. Bhanu's dying Hamlet says, '*Et tu, Horatio – traitor – con ... sp... irat ... or.*'

'After a decade of the presentation of *Hamlet*, I met Reeta Sondhi, a leading theatre critic, who was (initially) critical of my ending of the play (and now) agreed with my interpretation. She admitted that in the murky atmosphere of contemporary politics, friendship is used as a camouflage of deception to climb up the political ladder,' reveals Bhanu. 'After a fortnight or so the Royal Shakespeare Company from London ... (staged) its production of *Hamlet* in Delhi. A comparison between my production and the Royal Shakespeare Company's production was inevitable. Most of the discerning audience of Delhi appreciated my production for its dramatic sweep, depth, contemporary ring and the portrayal of (the character of) Hamlet as a highly sensitive, idealistic young man out of tune in a morally degenerate, gloomy and bloody world.'

Discussing about his cast, Bhanu said that he was very much pleased with the performance of his cast which consisted of Rajendra Jaspal as King Claudius, Neelam Mansingh Chowdhry as Queen Gertrude of Denmark, Om Puri as Prince Hamlet, Jyoti Deshpande as Ophelia and Harjeet Sindhu as Laertes. Pankaj Kapoor and Annu Kapoor played the roles of grave diggers.

This production is significant in the history of Hindi theatre movement in more ways than one. It brought laurels to Bhanu as an imaginative and prospective director who could present a classic not as a museum piece but could interpret it in a new perspective; most members of the cast like Om Puri, Pankaj Kapoor and Annu Kapoor shone as bright stars on the horizon of Bollywood. Neelam Mansingh Chowdhry today is a leading theatre director.

Sub Rang did not last long. Kirti Jain's production of Mridula Garg's *Party* was its second production and its swan song. The organisers went their separate ways.

Bhanu wanted to discover new theatrical areas to experiment, to move from one place to another and observe people and society, take risks and try out novel ideas. He was invited by Ranjeet Kapoor to see his collage, a stage presentation of poems, staged by Meghdoot, Lucknow. There were writers, painters and theatre lovers like Krishna Narayan Kakkar, literary critic and a promoter of performing arts and painter Ranbir Singh Bisht, who were associated with Meghdoot and wanted to stage Bhuwaneshwar Prasad's play *Sikandar*. The play was discussed at a meeting and Bhanu was also invited to take part in the discussion. Bhuwaneshwar's short plays were printed in a collection entitled *Carvan*.

Kakkar was a close friend of Bhuwaneshwar and wanted his plays to be staged. He writes, 'I tried twice to discuss Bhuwaneshwar's plays among theatre workers so that these could be staged. After ten or fifteen minutes (of) reading, the plays were dismissed on the ground that the dialogues are contrived.'

Bhanu had not heard about Bhuwaneshwar at the National School of Drama; even Nemichandra Jain had not mentioned him to the students. It was a great revelation for Bhanu. He decided to read the plays in the collection. 'I was so much engrossed in the reading of *Tambe Ke Kide* – one of the plays in the collection – that I read it again and over again in one sitting [*sic*] ... I went straight to meet Kakkar along with my friends and expressed my ardent desire to direct *Tambe Ke Kide*. I was also sorry that a play with so much dramatic possibilities remained unknown to theatre people,' recalls Bhanu.

Meghdoot had no funds; it was solely dependant on the donations of theatre lovers of Lucknow and there were organisational problems as well. A determined Bhanu took up the challenge and went ahead with his rehearsals. It was an irony that a writer who was said to be the pioneer of short plays in Hindi had never had his plays staged before. In the words of Kakkar, 'When Bhanu started working on *Tambe Ke Kide*, he began to discover new vitality and meaning in it. His amazement became all the more deep to find that Bhuwaneshwar conceptualised a play that rightfully belongs to the Theatre of the Absurd (as early as) in 1946 when Ionesco and Beckett did not appear on the world stage.'

After overcoming many hurdles, including the apathy of those theatre people of the town who had rejected Bhuwaneshwar's plays, *Tambe Ke Kide* was finally staged at Bal Rabindralay on 28 April 1975.

'There was great excitement. The production took the theatre world of Lucknow by storm. Leading personalities of literature and theatre were present. Raghuveer Sahay, the editor of *Dinman*, came all the way from Kanpur to attend the show which made a deep impression on him. He carried a scene of the play on the cover page of *Dinman* dated 25 May 1975, with my article on *Tambe Ke Kide* and Bhuwaneshwar's another play *Azadi ki Need* [*sic*],' says Bhanu.

A pioneer of new drama in Hindi, a fiction writer and poet, Bhuwaneshwar was influenced by Henrik Ibsen (1828-1906) and Bernard Shaw (1856-1950). But he never followed a beaten track. Munshi Prem Chand, the great Hindi novelist who published Bhuwaneshwar's works in his magazine *Hans*, commented on him—'Bhuwaneshwar has talent, depth, compassion and the power to express the right thing and a style of expression that stirs the human soul.'

Bhuwaneshwar felt that the new drama did not claim to answer questions nor did it accept that a question had a definite universal answer and was correct in all contexts. He did not attach any value to a play which was not written for the stage. The genius that he was, he departed from the concept of a play that was based on a love triangle. In the words of Nemichandra Jain: 'His dramatic sensibility and vision are very sharp and insightful. He has done unique experiment (with) the construction of the play and dramatic dialogue in his works. His understanding of life is deep and creatively innovative.'

Bhuwaneshwar depicted a world that was disintegrating and had lost its unifying force but the picture of that world he projected was grotesque, tinged with the elements of tragedy, comedy and laughter. It provoked and had a sense of horror. The audience did not identify itself with the characters whose motives were mysterious and unexplained. These are precisely the elements the Theatre of the Absurd manifests. In providing such a concept in 1946, Bhuwaneshwar was far ahead of his times and remained neglected by not only stage directors but also by Hindi literary critics. It goes to the credit of Bhanu to have discovered an Indian playwright belonging to the genre of the Theatre of the Absurd who wrote before the term the 'Theatre of the Absurd' became universally known. Bhanu was also the first to discover Hindi playwright Mani Madhukar when he directed his *Ras-Gandharva* for the Repertory Company of NSD. Again, he was the first to direct Doodh Nath's *Yum Gatha* in 1990.

❧

Discussing *Tambe Ke Kide*, it does not follow the concept of three unities—time, place and action. It has no logical story to tell and through dialogue remarkable for its theatricality and allegorical element, the play presents the human situation in the Indian context with poetic imagery. Other elements include grotesqueness and the comic—with a tinge of tragedy. Here our sense of well-being is shattered, reinforcing the fear of loneliness. We are reminded of the inevitability of death. A character says, 'Death sings lullaby to us beside our pillows.' There are images of terror, disillusionment and metaphysical anguish. Mechanical senselessness is symbolically conveyed by *Tambe Ke Kide* (copper germs). One voice says, 'Our latest invention is the *sooter* (sweater) of glass. Only the germs of copper (*tambe ke kide*) can eat them up. (Pause...) Our latest invention is of the germs of copper. These germs speak when you speak to them; they laugh when you evoke laughter ... the germs of copper.' The announcer speaks just before concluding the play with a song and announces, 'In my opinion the writer of the play is neurotic ... the whole play has no meaning. The playwright is trying to confuse (us).'

To stage such a play is indeed a challenging task for any director. Bhanu discovered in it a great deal of theatrical possibilities. The multi-dimensional medium of the stage provided him with the opportunity to create theatrical poetry to reflect boredom, tiredness, disillusionment, terror, neurotic behaviour and absurdity of the human condition.

The performers were in outlandish costumes. A bicycle was placed in the centre with its two wheels in an upward position and the rider lay on his back, turning the paddles with his feet.

Bhanu remembers, 'Not much liberty was taken with the script in this presentation. I have added four clowns as accompaniments. I conceived the entire play in small units complete in them. The encounter between these units and their dialectical relationship created the dramatic tension and that to my mind was the high point of the production. I did not use much of stage props. Only four wooden blocks were used and the play was in black-and-white to reflect its intent….'

This was how Bhanu evaluated *Tambe Ke Kide* in the context of contemporary Indian theatre and drama:

'*Tambe Ke Kide* is totally Indian in its experience and expression while *Adhe Adhure* by Mohan Rakesh, *Tughlaq* by Girish Karnad and Badal Sircar's *Evam Indrajeet* tend to be Western in perception. The sensibility of Karnad's *Hayavadana*, which we call a great Indian modern play, is Western in thought. The ideology, content and craft of *Khamosh Adalat Jaari Hai* by Vijay Tendulkar are borrowed. In contrast, *Tambe ke Kide's* craft and content are not borrowed. I can say without any hesitation that Bhuwaneshwar is still unsurpassable not only in Hindi dramaturgy but also in modern Indian drama.'

Bhanu stayed in Lucknow for about a month. Ever since, he continued to have close contact with the literary and arts world of that city. He used to interact often with literary luminaries like Amritlal Nagar, Kunwar Narayan and Shrilal Shukla. He fondly remembered those days which offered him fulfilling and creative moments.

Meanwhile, Bhanu was invited by Seva Mandir, a socio-cultural organisation of Udaipur, Rajasthan to do two plays. Once again, he embarked on a new journey, at once exciting and challenging.

State of Emergency: artistic freedom in peril

Right to equality is an important right provided for in Articles 14,15,16,17 and 18 of the Constitution. It is the principal foundation of all other rights and liberties...

Fundamental Rights in India

'After reaching Udaipur I discussed the arrangements with the organisers and the participants about conducting the theatre workshop. As I started working on Mohan Rakesh's play ... Emergency was declared (in the country) on 25 June 1975, suspending elections, civil liberties and freedom of expression. I was disturbed and shocked" reminisces Bhanu Bharti. 'As far as Udaipur was concerned there was no resistance, especially on the part of a small community of theatre people. Trade unions affiliated to Left parties replaced their flags with that of INTUC, an affiliate of the ruling Congress Party, overnight. The Emergency laws did not allow any theatrical presentation without the script being cleared by censorship. I had to do things accordingly.

'As an artist and citizen I was vehemently opposed to the Emergency regime but was not in a position to stage any controversial play. I was being shadowed by plainclothesmen. To escape censorship I selected some classics with the undertone of criticism of the power-hungry despotic rulers, employing allegorical means to express my anguish. Officials cleared these scripts with minor changes. However, we were allowed to proceed with our workshop and the staging of plays without official interference.'

Emergency repression was brutal in states like West Bengal, Andhra Pradesh, Bihar and some eastern parts of Uttar Pradesh. Some theatre activists in those states committed to radical ideology were arrested under DIR. There are works like Sudhir Mishra's film *Hazaaron Khwaishein Aisi* which revolves round Emergency and the growth of Naxalite movement during this period. Emergency abuses that affected the life of people in a small village are depicted in the Hindi novel *Katra Bi Aarzoo* by Rahi Masoom Raza. *Prisoners of Conscience*, a film made by Anand Patwardhan in 1978 highlights the plight of people robbed of their fundamental rights guaranteed by Article 19 of the Constitution.

Udaipur has witnessed just a few modern theatrical productions like Mohan Maharishi's *Shuturmurg* before Bhanu Bharti started the theatre workshop. This did not mean that there was no theatrical activity earlier. Shail Choyal, a well-known painter and theatre artist based in Udaipur describes theatrical activities in the town. 'My father', he says, 'veteran painter P.N. Choyal, used to write mostly one act plays. We had no directors as such. It was limited to club type activities [*sic*]. Doctors, engineers and 'office goers' were involved in the theatre. Dr Mohan Singh Mehta, an educationist and diplomat had formed Seva Mandir, donating his lifetime earnings to Seva Mandir, which became an instrument for social and cultural resurgence. Under the auspicies of Seva Mandir a dramatic society started functioning. Bhanu's arrival, his style of working, conducting workshops and handling of performers was an eye-opener for us,' says Choyal, who with his painter wife were active participants in the workshop. Bharat Ratna Bhargava, a playwright and theatre scholar, also joined them. Beena Kak, who rose to become the tourism and culture minister of Rajasthan later and joined films in 2005, also contributed to Bhanu's theatre production.

Bhanu designed his stage on an open field with mountains as a backdrop. It was a most befitting time to stage *Ashadh Ka Ek Din.* The rains were yet to come. The organisers had their reservations about presenting the play in the open as it required more money and special electrical arrangements. 'On the opening night it started to drizzle. We thought it would soon start raining heavily and our efforts might go waste. But it stopped and the show went on,' remembers a participant in that production.

'It was the first major production of a contemporary play in Udaipur, which was welcomed with a sense of great jubilation and (it) continues to be a milestone in the theatre movement of Rajasthan. For the first time the audience bought tickets for the show; the cost of each ticket was ₹ 2. At times more than a thousand people watched the play. We the theatre workers of the city were exposed to ... professional play production. For the first time we heard technical terms like "blocking" and "preparing for characterisation". Bhanu was a strict disciplinarian. Previously, our rehearsals were marred by unnecessary talks and gossips.[*sic*] Bhanu introduced an element of seriousness in our workshops and rehearsals,' remembers Choyal. Some theatre activists of the town who were cast in the play were Shrish Sharma as Kalidas, Chandralekha as Mallika, Surjit Kaur Choyal as Ambika and Beena Kak as Priyanka Manjari.

With the tremendous success of *Ashadh Ka Ek Din* Bhanu was requested to produce another play. This time he selected *Guinea Pig* by Mohit Chattopadhyay. In this play there are four characters. Structurally it is an avant garde work in which the character of Raja symbolises state power as an exploiter and a despotic ruler. He is opposed by a youth who represents the revolutionary forces. The conflict between the oppressed and the oppressor is reflected in a dialectical manner.

Two major directors had interpreted it differently. Rajendra Nath changed the denouement of the play, which he did for *Abhiyan* in 1972, ending his version 'perhaps on a defeatist note'. Another version of the play was by Bibhas Chakrabarty which he produced for Theatre Workshop in Kolkata as *Rajrakta* in 1971. In that version the oppressor – the Raja Sahib – is ultimately killed by the rebels.

Here the protagonist is a youth. Bhanu was inspired by the youth movement of 1968 and was actively involved in youth politics of his state (Rajasthan). Young as he was, he gave a radical interpretation to the script, underlining the victory of youth and the oppressed against status quo, tyranny, exploitation and totalitarianism. In the words of Mohit Chattopadhyay, who wrote this play in the backdrop of the Naxalite movement in Kolkata during 1970-'71 and the state repression, 'the Raja Sahib in the play represents autocracy which keeps the people as puppets. He appears in a variety of roles—as the head of the family (the autocratic paterfamilias), as a teacher bullying the students, as the political leader manipulating the masses, as the businessman cheating the people ... and this brought forth the all-round desperate urge to destroy "thick autocracy" (and) to rebel against it.'

In the words of Bhanu the production was highly appreciated by the audience. Leading personalities of the town congratulated him. 'But suddenly I had to confront the district collector,' says Bhanu. 'He said, "How have you staged a political play where there is Emergency?" [*sic*] I informed him that as required by the authorities I had got the script approved by the concerned officers. The collector was angry but did not take any action. In fact, the officials were unable to read between the lines; they made some cuts here and there but these were insignificant and in no way diluted the ideological content of the play. Due to the political content of the play, its presentation was not allowed in some places, especially in Tripura where it was virtually banned by the authorities'.

Now it was time for Bhanu to move to another city; to work with new artists, to confront creative challenges. At that time it did not occur to him that Udaipur would be his home and crucial to his artistic development in the context of contemporary Indian theatre. Here he met his would-be wife Chandralekha who played the role of Mallika in *Ashadh Ka Ek Din*.

At Udaipur, he was given an important assignment of establishing the University Institute of Dramatic Arts with provision for undergraduate and postgraduate courses in the field of theatrical arts, both theoretical and applied. After thoroughly studying the syllabi of leading Indian and foreign dramatic institutions he submitted a detailed report to the

University Grants Commission and Jaipur University for approval and grant of necessary funds. Meanwhile, he was instrumental in starting a part time certificate course in drama as a prelude to the opening of a full-fledged dramatic institute. The year was 1977. The Emergency continued in the country.

Bhanu organised a drama festival to make people drama conscious and watch for themselves the power of dramatic arts. The plays featured at the festival were *Jasma Oden, Andha Yug, Tambe Ke Kide, Hanush, Panchwan Sawar, Mitti Ki Gadi* and *Azadi Ki Neend.* As mandatory during the Emergency, all these plays were subjected to the scrutiny of the authorities for approval and that was obtained with negligible changes.

Bhanu tried to highlight the inherent social message in these modern classics. As far as Shanta Gandhi's *Jasma Oden* was concerned a song '*Raja Ka Kaat Dala Jaal, Majdoor Bhai Hoshiyar*' (The trap set out by the king has been destroyed; workers be on their guard against him) sent out a strong social message. This song was written by Bharat Ratna Bhargava and the play concluded with its forceful rendition. Bhanu had also recreated the confrontation between the king and workers. In this confrontation the workers encircle the king and finally destroy him. More than forty performers were cast in this production with Ila Arun in the lead.

'To me Dharamvir Bharati's *Andha Yug* and Bhavabhuti's *Mricchakatika* are political plays,' Bhanu explains. *Mricchakatika (Mitti Ki Gadi)* by Bhavabhuti exhorts the oppressed to rebel against a corrupt and tyranical regime. The play written around seventh century AD is strikingly contemporary in thought. Bhuwaneshwar Prasad's *Azadi Ki Neend* is a political farce that seeks to present the distorted view of freedom filled with vested interests, forcing the poor to rot in povery and live in perpetual slavery of the ruling class.

Bhanu's presentation of these festival plays was indeed a bold and courageous step and represents his struggle as an artist against the Emergency.

Apart from the drama festival, Bhanu organised a seminar on the Challenges of Contemporary Indian Theatre in which leading theatre personalities, including Sarveshwar Dayal Saxena, Kavita Nagpal, Kanhaiya Lal Nandan, Bhishm Sahni, Nemi Chandra Jain, Nand Kishore Acharya and Madan Mohan Mathur participated.

While the plans for the opening of the University of Dramatic Arts in Jaipur were to receive a formal approval, Bhanu developed an inner urge to leave Jaipur. This time he decided to travel beyond the borders of India. With his departure, plans for the University of Dramatic Arts were shelved and in its place a small dramatics department started under Jaipur University.

To Japan and back

The chief characters in these stories - the madman, Kung I-chi, Jun-tu, Ah Q and the rest - are all unfortunates in an abnormal society. Lu Hsun made a strong protest against their unhappy fate, and mercilessly exposed and attacked the forces that oppressed them, at the same time giving true expression to their wishes, demands and potential strength. He showed that the only way out was through changing society—through revolution.

—Feng Hsueh-Feng (*Lu Hsun: His Life and Works*)

Bhanu Bharti wanted to expand the horizon of his knowledge of traditional and classical theatre of Asia. He was particularly interested in the theatre of Indonesia and China but it was difficult to travel there. He got an opportunity to visit Japan to study the theory and undertake practical training in Japanese classical theatre forms—Noh and Kabuki. On 2 October 1977 he set out for Japan and stayed there for one and a half years.

For six months Bhanu was in Osaka University to study Japanese language and then he came to Nihon Daigaku, University of Tokyo where he practised and studied the two distinct forms—Noh and Kabuki. 'It was an interesting time,' recalls Bhanu. 'Japan had just started emerging as an economic power. Its currency was challenging (the) American dollar and capitalism (was) gaining strength. Commercialisation was changing the concept of artistic creation. Japan's great film maker Akira Kurosawa was not able to get funds; out of desperation he made an unsuccessful attempt to commit suicide. Finally Twentieth Century Fox Film Corporation came to his assistance to produce *Impersonator* ... But the attitude of the corporate sector was encouraging towards the performing and plastic arts. Every business house had a special space for performers and art galleries. As far as experimental works were concerned the funds were only provided by universities.

'Despite (the) tremendous industrial growth of Japan, during my stay there I found the attitude of (the) Japanese society conservative and industrics nurturing old feudal values of royalty to serve their own interests. For a worker his factory was his world. The only way out to rise to higher echelons of management was by marrying the daughter of (the) boss. Women at home were a picture of humility. Girls and boys in universities were a segregated lot. There was no concept of dating. Now the situation might have changed.'

Bhanu not only observed Japanese people and society but also devoted his time to the study and practice of the theatre. He saw almost all kinds of theatre—classical, experimental as well as modern and thoroughly studied the dramatic theory of Zen Zeami Motokiyo called *Kadensho*. It is the second treatise on the art of theatre in Asia after Bharata's *Natya Shastra*. Zeami (1363-1443) was an actor playwright who had left his imprint on the growth of Kabuki.

During his stay at the international hostel, Bhanu interacted with young people from different countries who had come here for studies. 'I got a chance to stay and interact with the young people from all over the world; particularly rewarding was the experience of meeting young students from the Middle East, Eastern Europe, East Asia, South-East Asia, Africa and Thailand. It was indeed an enriching and rewarding experience. I heard the accounts of (the) suffering of sensitive people from these different countries. I also witnessed the process of dehumanisation of a society at the hands of (the) ruling class and the vulgar market-driven economy. I also witnessed the distortion of a culture by the emerging merchant class with enough money to spend on their entertainment.'

Bhanu presents his observation of the Japanese theatre scene during his stay there in the following words:

'Remarkable for their costumes which are rich in colour and fabric, masks, refined dance and themes drawing mainly from Japanese classical literature and war experience of military nobility, people today who are above the age of sixty mainly go to witness Noh Theatre.

'Kabuki is another classical theatre form of Japan ... commercial in character. It is lively and replete with sentimentality. People above forty ... prefer to watch Kabuki theatre (for) entertainment. Tickets for Kabuki are expensive and the house mostly remains full.

'There is another form of theatre called Shingaiki where young people go. It is commercial and realistic (but) its productions are often shoddy, mainly aimed to entertain its patrons.

'Post-World War II, the Leftist ideology among young people became strong and the students' movement in 1968 spread all over the world and contributed to the growth of this movement in Japan. They have their specific theatre called *Red Tent—Aaka Tento*. To counter the influence of *Red Tent* among young students, another theatre, *Kura Tento – Black Tent* – emerged, propagating Rightist ideology and denouncing Leftist movement. This underground Marxist theatre was developed into a vibrant new form with dance and modern popular music. But severe police repression had almost suppressed and destroyed this form of political theatre.

'Apart from classical and new Japanese theatre, there is an array of different styles of theatre performances in Tokyo. In Noh, masks are used and the body of (the) performer is covered; it hinders natural movement but the performers float within the costumes. This is how the animate is transformed into inanimate, creating a new form of animation. In other words it is a process of transforming living into non-living and back to living. It was a great experience for me. Tension is ... created while the subtle process of this transformation takes place.

'Watching Bunraku is a wonderful experience. The oldest Japanese theatre style known since the seventh century is called Puppet Theatre but I do not accept it as just puppet theatre. It is a complex art form which blends stories and intricacies of puppeteers. Both (the) puppet and puppeteers are in front of the audience. One puppet is handled by three puppeteers; the head puppeteer manipulates the head and the right hand of the puppet and the second one handles the left hand and properties and the third puppeteer handles (the) legs of the puppet. The head puppeteer does not wear masks and is in formal dress. But the two (other) puppeteers are in black hood. There is remarkable coordination between them; there is such a harmony and synchronisation between them that they even (breathe) in unison. The face of the head puppeteer remains expressionless while the puppet laughs and weeps and makes movements. The performances are mostly melodramatic. The puppeteers do not betray any human emotions and puppets – which are in half human size – are charged emotionally. Right in front of our eyes the puppets enact (a) drama which is so vivid, life-like and engrossing that we forget the presence of the puppeteer who manipulates them. Minimal props are used which enables us to … focus on the puppets.

'A great deal of training and patience are required to master this technique generally performed by a hereditary class; the training starts from childhood. This is a wonderful theatre; it is not a theatre for children but a theatre for adults. I have imbibed several elements from Bunraku. Our urban actor's trained realistic style cannot adopt this technique. That is why I went to work with Bheels who understand this kind of theatre and act. Some of the elements of Bunraku are used in *Katha Kahi Ek Jale Ped Ne, Aks-Tamasha* and *Ab Garibi Hatao*.'

Having exposed himself to the classical and modern theatre of Japan with practical training in classical forms, Bhanu was full of enthusiasm. He wanted to use the elements of Japanese theatre to create a new contemporary Indian theatre and in the process help evolve a new theatre idiom.

As he returned to India and Delhi he was welcomed by his friends and lovers of an innovative Indian theatre form. Sarveshwar Dayal Saxena, Archana Verma, Dinesh Agarwal and a few other friends founded Rang Peeth. It made its entry to the Delhi theatre scene with Sarveshwar Dayal Saxena's play *Ab Garibi Hatao* under the direction of Bhanu Bharti with music by B.V. Karanth. A political satire, Bhanu incorporated the elements of Bunraku. Traditional puppeteers in black costumes from Shadipur Depot were invited to participate in the production. They manipulated the characters of politicians in power. The impoverished masses were shown crouching on the stage.

Satish Katyal and Meera Mishra played the roles of Nat and Nati respectively. The play was staged at AIFACS. In spite of the fact that the form was innovative, the production could not leave a deep impact on the audience because the script was sketchy with overtones of journalese.

After the Emergency came to an end on 21 March 1977, Janta Party came to power at the Centre and the experiment to combine different political conflicts with different ideologies led by regional and small-time leaders into a ruling party failed. Indira Gandhi's Congress came to power with Indira Gandhi as the Prime Minister. Bhanu was impressed with an English translation of a Japanese short story—*A Tale Told by a Scorched Tree*. He himself adapted it in Hindi and produced it under the banner of Rang Peeth as *Katha Kahi Ek Jale Ped Ne*.

It is the story of a monkey queen who wants to defy death to obtain immortality. A stage comes when she becomes haggard and aged, her body and face metamorphose into ugly and dreadful forms. People came to see her, but she refuses to meet them and her attendant shows them her portrait of her youthful days. Ultimately the queen dies a natural death and with her death her empire is wiped out.

The metaphor is a severe criticism of fascism—of a despotic ruler destroying democratic institutions to realise his or her dictatorial designs.

Bhanu designed his production in open air. There was a thirty feet high platform for the dramatic action of the queen and on the ground the crowd scenes were enacted with human performers giving the illusion of monkeys.

'I wanted to give this production an epic dimension with a vast expanse,' Bhanu says. 'That was possible in an open environment. I did not want to create realistic monkeys. So I discovered a new body language. A lot of time was devoted to improvise speech pattern and physical movements. Imitating monkeys' style of speech and their mannerism would have become artificial and it would have diluted the content. At the same time, I did not want my performers to act like humans while playing the role of monkeys. My actors had no make-up and no masks; they had no tails and were in brown tights. What I asked them (to do) was to imbibe the monkeys' physical characteristics—in the uncanny way they stood, moved and expressed themselves. This worked wonderfully. There was a large cast with Sindhu Mishra in the lead role of the Monkey Queen.

'The audience described it as a memorable experience in an experimental theatre with bold political interpretation of a Japanese tale with universal message. The Press gave rave reviews, giving their own interpretation of the *Monkey Queen*.'

During the phase of the early 1980s one of the most talked about productions of Bhanu was *Chandrama Singh Urf Chamku* which he did for the second year students of The National School of Drama in May 1982. Adapted from the original story by Lu Hsun, father of new Chinese literature, the story is written against the backdrop of the 1911 revolution in China, which failed because the peasants were not mobilised. The central character Ah Q is the object of feudal exploitation. In the words of contemporary Chinese writer Feng Hseur-Feng '...in the continuous clash between Ah Q and his oppressors, Ah Q himself is torn between submission and revolt, and has always an urge to revolt. Ah Q, like all the oppressed can liberate himself only by smashing his fetters – by revolution – and this strength he does possess ...' In Bhanu's adaptation Ah Q becomes Chandrama Singh and a village in Unnav, Uttar Pradesh became the locale which witnessed a surge of the Naxalite movement. 'I took the students to that village and acquainted them with the lifestyle of the people there and explained to them the antagonistic forces (at play) there and the apalling condition of landless farmers,' says Bhanu.

Bhanu designed his production in the open, projecting a whole village. The style of design and acting were based on socialistic realism. Structurally, the script was episodic with small units. The action between different sequences was juxtaposed at times for heightening the dramatic effect.

'It was a production on an epic scale aimed at bringing to the fore the social antagonism and misery of the protagonist and his dilemma in a feudal society. Though it was a production for second year students, other students' classes were also involved.'

Despite this artistic fete, the production created conflict among the students. 'Because of the internal politics, attempts were made to spoil the production,' reflects Bhanu. 'First I was branded as a Congress stooge; when that failed some students were instigated by vested interests in the school to create violent scenes in the course of rehearsals. Once a group of students came drunk in the rehearsals and created scenes of hooliganism. I was forced to report the matter to director B.M. Shah and the school had to suspend six students. The rehearsals however, went on smoothly and the show was a great success. More than 40 students participated in the production with Vipin Sharma in the lead role of Chandrama Singh.'

'Bhanu directed *Chandrama Singh Urf Chamku* for the National School of Drama Repertory Company also in 1985, casting experienced and talented actors with Raghuvir Yadav in the leading role of Chandrama Singh. The device of juxtaposition of contrasting moods and situations produced the most profound emotional impact on the audience. The presentational style was similar to what he followed in the 1982 production. A severe comment on the inhuman face of a semi-feudal polity, it was a memorable theatrical piece rarely seen in Delhi'.

Bhanu joined Shri Ram Centre as an Art Director. His participation in Natya Samaroh in 1984 organised by Sangeet Natak Akademi for young directors along with his production of *Pashu Gayatri* in Mewari catapulted him to national fame and his highly creative experimental works came to the notice of the nation.

Gavari: the Bheel theatre

For in India, we have to begin almost at the beginning and come full circle if we are to build up an indigenous tradition rooted in the soil and in the consciousness of our people. They have remained, despite all the civilising process they have undergone and despite the sophisticated classical city dramas, the custodians of certain elemental forms. No sudden leap into the future can be attempted, but we can advance only if we develop a national drama rather than a superficial smart middle class comedy, borrowed from the West.

—Mulk Raj Anand

But with the new interest in the traditional theatre we cannot ignore the fact that for example folk theatre is not only regarded as a medium through which to depict a plebeian way of life and a realistic view of historical factors; there is also a growing body of opinion that tends to treat it as a purely folklore affair whereby myths and rituals are stripped of their historical and social relevance.

—Fritz Benniwitz

Bhanu Bharti is an artist endowed with an intense desire to experiment to recreate something new and relevant to the Indian situation, something living and vibrant. He had explored Western and Japanese theatre, both classical and traditional. In 1975 he had a chance to watch a 4000-year-old tribal theatre performance while he was conducting a workshop in Seva Mandir at Udaipur.[1] 'I heard the beat of madal – the brass plate – with an irresistible quality. Participants in the workshop told me that these instruments are accompaniments of a theatre performance called Gavari, a Bheel theatre. I went to watch it. The Bheels were enacting their drama at the crossroads of the Seva Mandir. I saw some of it but it impressed me. I thought it needs an in-depth study to understand this Bheel theatre [*sic*]', recalls Bhanu. This minor incident gradually became his ruling passion to discover elements of a living contemporary indigenous Indian theatre.

When he came back from Japan he decided to make a documentary on Gavari. He spent money from his own pocket on this project. 'I am yet to recover the money I had spent on the production of this film,' Bhanu says. But far from being discouraged from this setback he became all the more determined to work on Gavari.

As an art director of the Shri Ram Centre for Arts and Culture, Delhi, he was provided with an opportunity to work on his dream project. In 1984 Sangeet Natak Akademi (SNA) launched a scheme for assistance to young theatre workers with the broad objective of supporting and sustaining the creative efforts and energies of young enterprising theatre workers. This was indeed a laudable scheme of SNA. Promising and highly-talented directors like Bhanu, Prasanna, Bansi Kaul and Ratan Thiyam sought 'inspiration in the traditional/folk theatre forms, and thus through a process of artistic cross-fertilisation with modern sensibilities (helped) contemporary theatre assimilate the heritage of the past.'[2]

Unfortunately, this vibrant theatre form of the Bheels of Rajasthan is hardly known outside the state. Even in Rajasthan the feudal aristocracy and urban elite treated this form with indifference if not with disdain. Thanks to the Bharatiya Lok-Kala Mandal, Udaipur and its founder director Devilal Samar and scholars like Dr Mahendra Bhanawat, the attention of the literary circle of Rajasthan was drawn. Though we know about the Rajasthani folk forms like the Khyal, Swang and Leela it is a pity that little is known about the powerful Bheel theatre form Gavari.

1. *Loknatya Gavari: Udbhav Aur Vikas* by Dr Mahendra Bhanavat – P 20
2. From Brochure issued by Sangeet Natak Akademi at Natya Samaroh 1984

By discovering Gavari and creatively experimenting with it to create a new contemporary Indian theatre, Bhanu has immensely contributed to a new perspective for Indian theatre, displaying the tremendous possibilities of exploring Gavari as a dynamic theatre form.

As a product of a tribal society which is comparatively free from the commodification of its traditional art forms belonging to its people and created by their collective sensibility and the social relationship among the people based on equality, the evolution of Gavari as an artistic form offers exciting anthropological study. But this study is beyond the scope of the present project which mainly deals with the dissection of theatrical elements of Gavari, the social relations of tribal people and the place of Gavari in their lives against the background of Bhanu's exploration of Gavari. An outline of the evolution of Gavari, the socio-economic condition of the Bheels of Rajasthan and the theatrical expressive elements in Gavari are essential to understand the enduring appeal of Gavari and its dramatic grandeur.

Said to be once rulers in certain parts of Rajasthan, Gujarat and Madhya Pradesh, the history of Bheels starts from sixth century AD. However, Gavari is part of the socio-cultural life of Bheels living in Udaipur, Doongarpur and Banswada areas. They are brave and love their freedom. They prefer to die rather than surrender to their enemy. In the history of Rajasthan they are treated with respect. When Maharana Pratap was engaged in a fiery guerrilla battle against the mighty force of Emperor Akbar, the Bheels supported him. 'The Bheels were given due recognition by the Rajputs which was expressed in the inclusion of the figure of the Bheel chief on one side of the state emblem of Mewar while the other side showed Maharana Pratap, the fort of Chittor form the central part of their emblem. The same was true of the erstwhile Kulshalgarh state.'[3] Several Rajput chiefs are known to have displayed their honour for the Bheels.

The forces of British imperialism were unable to subdue this brave race; they miserably failed to extend their domination to the regions controlled by Bheels maintaining their non-exploitative primitive

3. *People of India* by D.K. Samanta, P 151

social framework. Bheels bravely thwarted the inhuman assaults by princely rulers of Rajasthan. They are highly conscious of their dignity and cultural identity. They would prefer to die of hunger rather than beg. They are brave, revengeful, fearless but good natured.

After Independence there has not been radical transformation in the social structure of the Bheel society. The unimaginative economic and administrative policy imposed by an apathetic bureaucracy and the process of brahmanisation and *Bhagwat* movements have not improved the social condition of Bheels who are today a poor lot. Marginal farmers as they are, new forest laws have deprived them of their rights to meet their bare needs from the forests. The literacy rate of Bheels in Rajasthan is as low as 7 per cent. Most of them have become landless and forced to work as construction workers to make a living. Swaroop Dass, a 'bhopa' (tribal priest at the village temple and usually an influential leader) of a Bheel village, portrays a pathetic picture of Bheel tribes in these words—'We have been debarred from entering the forests; we cannot collect fodder for cattle and wood for cooking meals. We are not allowed to hunt; nor can we go to the forest to collect honey—these were the main sources of our livelihood which we have been using for centuries. Now our bow and arrow have become a mere antique piece. Our young people are condemned to work as cheap labour on construction sites. You will not hear beautiful tribal songs from their lips. They have stopped singing and dancing—qualities a Bheel child imbibes from his parents and the soil.'

Bhopa assumes a pivotal position in the Bheel society, a force which brings unity and order and reflects the collective ideas of the community. He is a philosopher, friend, spiritual guide and physician. At the time of crisis the community goes to him for guidance. Bhopa is a hereditary institution which evolved when the ruling class has not emerged in the homogenous collective whole of the primitive society. Despite changes in the social structure the bhopa continues to evoke a sense of reverence and awe. When he dies his body is buried, though Bheels cremate their dead. A temple is built at the site of his grave; the dead in Bheel society are treated as gods because of religious beliefs, signifying society's deep reverence for their ancestors. Though Bheel women are not permitted to participate in the religious rituals, they enjoy more freedom in the matter of marriage and social intercourse.

The agriculture in the Bheel villages depends on rain; the lakes – which were once water reservoirs – are gradually drying up. People often face acute water shortage and drought.

The brief sketch of the Bheel society is essential to understand Gavari which is the part of the superstructure of a predominantly agrarian society with primitive characteristics. In this primitive setting man surrenders to nature, he believes in superstition, witchcraft and magic. This belief should not be denounced but it is the aesthetic impulse inherent in the primitive man and takes the form of artistic expression. In the initial stage this expression reflects man's fear of natural phenomenon but in the ultimate analysis it manifests man's inner urge to control nature through his collective strength.

Some of the superstitions of Bheels are strange enough for outsiders. Bhanu narrates one such superstition. Whenever there is a famine, Bheels think the local moneylender has kept the clouds captive and confined in his locker with a view to trading in the misery of the starving people. To liberate these clouds they go to the moneylender's house with bows and arrows, break-open the locker and plunder all the valuables kept in the locker. Now moneylenders have become clever. Whenever there is a famine, they move all valuables from the locker and keep just a token amount of money along with a coconut.

As Bhanu combined the insight of an intellectual, creativity of a sensitive artist and finesse of a craftsman, he studied the Bheel cultural ethos, social milieu and various artistic modes of expression to grasp the array of theatrical elements inherent in Gavari. His objective was not to reproduce Gavari's form and content as projected by the Bheels. This would have been easy for any director ready to produce an exotic stuff as export commodity. Bhanu wanted to create a new and indigenous theatre idiom rooted in the consciousness of the people and reflecting contemporary sensibility. He took years to study this form and to identify himself with the Bheels, and then set up the Disha Natya Sansthan, Udaipur, with Bheel performers.

A brief description of Gavari, apart from its religious and ritualistic character as a form of total theatre experience, will give us some idea as to its contemporary relevance, its dynamic utility, freshness and enduring appeal. It is also important to identify theatrical elements in this centuries-old form which are identical with modern theories of theatrical art—epic, the theatre of Bertolt Brecht, realistic theatre of Stanislavski, the environmental theatre of Richard Schechner and so on. It is also important to know the basic differences between the Gavari and Bharat Muni's *Natya Shastra*.

Gavari was evolved initially as a ritualistic dance to worship Lord Shiva and his consort Gauri. Shiva is the god of Bheels and it is their belief that Gauri is their daughter. Once in a year in Bhadrapad (September – starting from Rakshabandhan), Gauri visits her parents, symbolising the warm and emotional reunion between daughter and her parents. Intricately woven into the fabric of this belief is the mythological story of Shiva and Bhasmasur. As a result of his hard ascetic propitiation, Bhasmasur was able to please Shiva and obtained from him the *bhasmi kada*, a bracelet, which bestowed unprecedented destructive power to the demon. He could reduce anyone to ashes the moment he put his hand with *bhasmi kada* on his or her head. Mad with his newly acquired limitless destructive power, Bhasmasur decided to reduce Shiva to ashes and took away Gauri to make her his wife. This created havoc in all the three lokas—Heaven, Earth and the Subterranean. Finally, Vishnu came to the rescue of Shiva to save the universe. He appeared before Bhasmasur in the form of Mohini, an embodiment of feminine beauty and eroticism and destroyed Bhasmasur with the *bhasmi kada* with which he was determined to finish Shiva. Before dying Bhasmasur was able to get a boon from Vishnu that he should be remembered by people. Vishnu assured him that he would be remembered through the performance of Gavari every year.

Gauri is the daughter of the Bheel. A religious celebration called Gauri is performed to welcome her. The Bheel performers visit the village where their daughters or sisters are married and they need not be invited by anybody. The moment they reach the village, they are welcomed by their daughters and sisters in accordance with the Bheel ritualistic tradition. Rayee is worshipped and the trishul of Gauri is erected, to the beat of tribal instruments. The women start singing a song called Bharat. The performers need no formal or makeshift stage and any crossroads or open space serves as their venue; the villagers gradually assemble in thousands. They sing through the night in the temple of Bholanath to seek his blessings for the welfare and security of the community and for a rich crop. In fact, the Bheels consider themselves part of the entourage of Shiva and (Hemajal) Himachal – Parvati's father – who is believed to be a Bheel.

Gavari starts at sunrise and comes to an end at sunset. It continues without any break, the action shifts to various places, the character of the thief hides himself on a branch of a tree, some characters enact their role on the terrace and some action takes place in another part of the village. The audience keeps shifting to the venue of action. In fact, the whole village becomes an action area crowded by a large number of villagers who come from far-off villages. As a symbol of Bheel cultural identity and social bonding, only Bheel tribes are allowed to perform Gavari; Bheel women are not allowed. As for the audience, the people of any caste, creed and religion can watch it. The performers are not actors; they completely identify themselves with their characters; they forget their real identity. For forty-five days they stop doing any manual work.

Since Gavari is basically a religious obeisance, the performers do not visit their homes. During the day they perform and at night they stay at the village temple. For forty-five days they do not change their clothes which are immersed after the festival is over and the entire village bids goodbye to their daughter Gavari who leaves for her husband's home. The performers live a pious life during Gavari, they do not eat meat and green vegetables, do not drink alcohol and maintain celibacy. Not only the performers but the entire village stops eating non-vegetarian food. In a mixed village in which apart from Bheels, other communities like Rajputs, Muslims and artisans follow a strict discipline in their day-to-day lives, to show their solidarity and bonding with the Bheel tribe. Every community contributes to the village management which looks after the food for the performers and makes their stay comfortable at the temple.

A personal experience of watching Gavari in a mixed population village – about 80 kilometres from Udaipur – in the company of Bhagwan Lal Kachhawa, an expert in Gavari theatre revealed certain interesting facts. Murad Begum and Lal Khan Pathan were among the audience. 'Our ancestors were here 200 years ago. During Gavari we stop working and do not eat meat and we do whatever we can to serve the performers. We consider ourselves part of this community celebration,' said Murad Begum. Manji Ram, an octogenarian, and a village carpenter said, 'I have been making wooden masks for the character of Bhasmasur.' Similarly, the village potter has a special role to play in the success of Gavari. He makes a huge elephant of clay for the finale which is immersed in the lake.

The colour of costumes conveys the social status and traits of the characters; they are scanty but help in characterisation and character identification. Mask is an important part of costumes.

As for the make-up a simple technique is used. The ingredients of the make-up include coal black, lime, red ochre, turmeric, indigo and ashes. Gavari is a theatre that could be described as a realism of a rough-hewn kind. It evokes a whole gamut of human emotions. The *rasa*s that are expressed are the ugly, the base, the horrible, the heroic, the comic, the lofty and the beautiful.

Music is the soul of this theatre replete with vibrant tribal dance, innumerable episodes from different sources—both mythological and social. Contemporary references are also incorporated into the structure of dramatic enactments. There is a unique style of blending these episodes through commentators. In a way this is a total theatre at its best conceived over the years by the collective genius of the Bheel tribes—isolated culturally, socially, economically and politically from what is called the mainstream.

The following are the main characters of Gavari. The character of Budhiya wears a mask, he symbolises Shiva and Bhasmasur. The mask is made of wood. He wears red shorts and holds a stick in his hand. At the upper end of this stick is tied a piece of red cloth. Budhiya moves four steps forward and four steps backward. He follows the reverse direction to what the dancers follow.

Budhiya is accompanied by two women characters (played by men) called Raeyeen who stand for Uma and Parvati. Some consider them as Parvati and Vishnu in the form of Mohini. Both these Raeyeeyan wear identical costumes, they speak simultaneously and move in unison to illustrate the fact that they have two bodies but one soul.

The show is conducted by the bhopa who is a medium for Shiva. He goes into a trance frequently as an indication of the entry of Lord Shiva into his body. He wears a string of small brass bells round his ankle and waist and holds a trident in his hand. Kutkudiyas are two important characters of Gavari who narrate a short history before a story begins to unfold. The repertoire of Gavari is vast. The mythological story of Amba and Shiva holds a special place in the repertoire. Stories like *Neema Ki Maa* are a commentary on society; even more contemporary themes are being incorporated but the core of the Gavari is essentially ritualistic, which continues to dominate the show.

According to Dr Mahendra Bhanawat, the characters could be placed in four categories—gods, humans, demons and animals. It is the man who assumes the pivotal place. He is all-powerful and with the help of superior skill and wisdom he has the capacity to shape his destiny. Even gods envy him and wish to be born as man. Man dominates all the creatures of the earth and this is Gavari's contemporary vision of man.

Gavari's dramatic splendour is revealed in its dialogue. In the words of Bhanu one of the most important features of Gavari is its dialogue. Contemporary playwrights should learn the craft of writing dialogue from the practitioners of Gavari.

The format of the Gavari stage is in a nebulous shape. There is an inner circle called Manak Chowk which is reserved for the gods. There is another circle in which the main characters move. The audience sits circling the actors' space and performers make their entry and exit through a demarcated area set at a distance.

Are there elements in Gavari that we find in contemporary theories of theatrical art?

On the surface Gavari appears to be close to Brecht's theory of epic theatre. Brecht talks of total theatre—music, singing, dance and masks and then between the changes of episodes there is a space for commentary to provide the audience with time to reflect on the dilemma of modern man living in an antagonistic world. This kind of device is called the alienation effect.

The basic aesthetics of Brechtian epic theatre is to avoid identification with the characters and to introduce elements of alienation. As far as Gavari theatre is concerned its use of the elements of total theatre are identical with that of epic theatre. But the spectators do not maintain distance from the characters; they are engrossed in them and, more often than not, go into trance.

The performer in the epic theatre tries to keep distance from the character he portrays. In Gavari the performers completely immerse themselves into the character; they are one and the same. However, Gavari performers do not treat theatre as an ivory tower. They are part of the community that sports Gavari. They are part of the superstructure of the tribal society; their craft comes to them as automatically and spontaneously as hunting, agricultural work and honey collection from the forest.

There are some elements in Gavari that are common to Richard Schechner's environment theatre. It is a kind of a site-specific theatre and achieves greater authenticity and audience engagement by staging its action in an appropriate and real world. Action in environmental theatre keeps changing from one real space to another with the audience following it. In Gavari the action transcends time, place and space; some episodes take place on terraces and some even on the branch of a tree (for example, to show a thief hiding there). In Gavari everything is spontaneous; there is nothing contrived as we watch in environmental theatre. In Gavari, dramatic sweep flows uninterruptedly in a dynamic way as if it springs from life itself.

Bharata's *Natyashastra* is an elaborate treatise on classical Sanskrit drama. Gavari is a tribal theatre with an unwritten art form. *Natyashastra* belongs to the highly articulate ruling class which seeks to perpetuate the class interest. The strength of Gavari lies in unwittingly violating the rules laid down by those living in ivory towers. Devi Lal Samar observes that the hero in Gavari is Bhasmasur, a demon, in the form of the character of Budiya. It shows tribal disdainful defiance of *Natyashastra*'s insistence that only a Brahmin or a Kshatriya of noble character can be cast as hero.

Gavari is a people's theatre—people who love their freedom and are ready to die for it. They are illiterate but proud of their cultural and historical heritage.

Bhanu has done a great service to contemporary Indian theatre by discovering Gavari, working with Bheels and presenting their theatre to the larger Indian audience with a new perspective and in modern idiom.

Pashu Gayatri: quest for new theatre idiom

When defining the subject of art, reference is made to the materialist resolution of the fundamental question of the theory of art—the question of art's relationship to reality, the co-relation between real life itself and its reflection in art. When viewed in this way content is tantamount to this or that phenomenon of life, and art to the specific form in which the phenomena is reflected.

—Avner Zis (*Foundations of Marxist Aesthetics*)

Bhanu Bharti's journey into the land of Bheels, his interaction with them, his deep understanding of their theatre Gavari and his collaboration with them to produce modern plays – creatively selecting elements from Gavari – are crucial to his artistic development. Reaching out to the Bheels was not akin to nurturing a fetish for tribal roots. For him it was the time to rediscover the roots of Indian theatre, the relationship between society and theatre and between rituals and theatre. It was a process of sorts, to unlearn what he had learnt.

On a hot and sunny day on 3 September 2007, Bhanu Bharti and the author reached Maudi village – 50 km from Udaipur – and were welcomed by the Bhopa. The surrounding Bheel performers offered cool, clean water to drink followed by curd – fresh and sweet – in a *katora* (metal bowl). The Bhopa commented, 'Soon the pure water and the curd, which we had in plenty, will become past luxuries because our water sources are drying up and we are not allowed to bring fodder from the forest for our cattle'.

An enlightening informal conversation began. Bhanu appeared to be quite at home in the company of the Bheel Gavari performers. Sugna, the main singer in *Amar Beej* was there too; he sang some songs from Gavari in a tuneful and powerful voice. Samp Dass describes his experience: 'We worked with Bhanuji for one-and-a-half months. He explained to us what we should do and how we should act on the stage. It was not difficult. We visited several places to present *Pashu Gayatri* and other plays. Wherever we performed we were welcomed with thunderous applause. In Goa the audience actually believed that one of our male members – playing a female role – was a young woman and were completely bewildered on knowing the truth. Our association with Bhanuji brought to our village a great deal of honour. We will not leave Bhanuji. He is not greedy, he is affectionate and affable. He comes to us often and we also go to Udaipur city to meet him."

These Bheel performers are very touchy and sensitive, though extremely hardworking and intelligent. Bhanu recounts one incident: 'It all happened in Goa. Dhanna was off tune; Dhalu pointed out his mistake and told him not to be casual. Dhanna was in underwear; he felt humiliated and left the venue in an angry mood. We were all worried about his safety. He was a stranger in the city with (a) language problem. After hours of search we could locate him, standing on a beach. When we requested him to return, he threatened that he would jump into the sea if we went near him. However, after a lot of persuasion he came back. This is one of the major differences between tribal performers and urban actors. For a tribal performer, character and actor are the same [*sic*]. Stage property – for example a piece of cloth to create the illusion of the sea – is not property but (the) sea for them. For them theatre is not illusion but a real one—the life and society [*sic*].' Bhanu believes that theatre – in order to be living – has to be part of social activity. Today in an urban milieu, the society is disintegrating. Neighbours are strangers to each other. In such a situation the concept of community to sustain theatrical art is absent. When Bhanu saw Gavari, he discovered that this is communal art. To him theatre, community and society are essential to promote theatrical activity of any kind. Gavari survives therefore, thanks to its unique roots and grows as an art form to reflect popular aspirations.

Another aspect that Bhanu was impressed by in Gavari was its ritualistic character. 'I observed that theatre which is purely entertainment is becoming irrelevant and disintegrating fast but the theatre which has its roots in some kind of ritual that a community believes in, is still thriving. I am talking of traditional theatre. What happened to Nautanki, Tamasha and Jatra which have no roots in community beliefs? When films appeared on the entertainment scene these forms gradually started disintegrating. On the contrary, the forms which have roots in community rituals did not crumble. For example Thiyyam in Kerela, Yaksagana in Karnataka, Thalkuttu in Andhra and Tamil Nadu, Kathakali in Kerela—these forms were not battered by cinema. This was my observation of traditional and folk forms (of theatre in) the country.

'The biggest question for me was the milieu and the kind of audience I (was) performing for. The urban society does not believe in rituals; it is … (an) agnostic group of isolated people. Even we have no faith in the marriage rituals; we have no faith in these ceremonies. So they have become empty, losing all meaning (and significance). The social fabric … (is) ruptured. It is not possible to live in a joint family. Even at the micro level when children grow up, they leave the family. In such a situation what kind of communal expression (remains) and how is it possible to manifest this expression? These were the challenges a creative person has to confront.

'To solve the problem of dichotomy between an alienated and disintegrated society, art, crisis in social life and cultural identity, I found (elements) in *Pashu Gayatri* and *Amar Beej* (which could) bridge the gap between the traditional and the modern. These two works of theatrical art are the result of deep interaction with the tribal artists. These are modern plays but had roots in Gavari and (are) performed by people rooted in the milieu … these are able to cut across the language and social barriers and invoke … a wonderful response all over the country.'

Bhanu is greatly fascinated with the power of music in Gavari. He realises that music is an important and integral part of Gavari and is sorry that in modern theatre, music is being increasingly ignored. In

Aks-Tamasha he used the device of theatre music with great success. He is of the opinion that to understand the significance of theatre music one should watch Gavari. Both the Gavari and *Pashu Gayatri* forms of theatre offer total theatre experience using space and time with great freedom. You will find the possibility of turning anything into a dramatic statement whether it is a bamboo stick or a piece of cloth.

Another feature that struck Bhanu is that in Gavari theatre the full body of the actor becomes a vehicle of expression whereas an urban actor gives emphasis only on his facial expressions. Modern theatre should imbibe this element from Gavari. There is free flow of space and time, which operate simultaneously. The Gavari actors have full faith in what they are doing. For them an actor in the role of a king is truly a king. This is not possible with the modern actor.

'These performers have full confidence in me. They know that I have great respect for their culture. They know that I trust them and in return, they trust me. I stayed with them, ate with them; we were very open to each other. My Communist background helped me identify myself with them. I learnt a great deal from them, especially their ability to relate with nature, with their surroundings and their strong bond with their people and community. They are very proud people. If you injure their pride, they retaliate violently. You will never find a Bheel begging or stealing. If he is caught in the act of stealing, the community outcasts him.

'While directing them I have not subjected them to vigorous discipline. It is challenging to ask them to follow playing time on a modern proscenium stage. But they have a broad sense of timing and stage compositions. The tribal performers are not dependent on the director. What I believe is that a director has no clear-cut role to play in a production because theatre is essentially the medium of the actor. But the presence of the director in a theatre would always be felt. While working with tribals as a director you have several roles to play: you cannot deal with them the way you deal (with) urban actors. Nor can you use them as puppets. You have to relate yourself with their socio-cultural beliefs to get work out of them. They are so authentic; no urban actor can match them. They react with guts and then the expression is superb. Urban artists understand art intellectually even if he is convinced that it is difficult to express through guts. There is always a gap between intellect and body.'

In the course of his observation of Gavari and his interaction with tribal artists in the production of *Pashu Gayatri* Bhanu has done a deep study of Brecht's epic theatre. According to Bhanu, 'Brecht has admitted that he has learned Asian and especially Chinese theatre to evolve his theory of the new kind of political theatre. The Asian element was incorporated to achieve his political aim but Gavari is not political theatre. It is episodic in character, though it does have a kind of alienation effect but this effect is different from what we perceive in Brecht. There is no dichotomy between actor and character in Gavari – they coexist. There is no question of the actor coming out of the character. Similarly, there is no duality between performer and the audience. In fact, Gavari contains religious content with political overtones; it has social satire and emotional appeal to create a social bonding'.

Another factor that captivates Bhanu is the starkness of the Gavari theatre. 'I have been trying to eliminate ornamental and superficial details,' he explains. 'I tried to capture the essence. That is why people say that my productions are bare, there is no miracle. I am trying to achieve in theatre the literary richness Kabir accomplished in poetry with simple and concise diction. This is very difficult, I am aware of this challenge. Whether it is music or performance there is simplicity in Gavari. It is direct and unassuming and yet it has such inner richness that it evokes man's deeper spiritual yearnings, stirring deep human emotions. This is the relevance of Gavari theatre at a time when the middle class has become self-centred. The urban art writer and critics have no tome to probe the rich spiritual reservoir of folk that contains the essence of the century's human experience and wisdom.'

❧

In the period 1985-'86 Bhanu established a repertory company with Bheel farmers. He named it *Disha Natya Sansthan*, Udaipur. Over the years Bhanu has done several productions with his Bheel cast.

Pashu Gayatri (1984), *Amar Beej* (1989-'90) and *Kaal Katha* (1987), which have become landmark theatrical works of art. Premiered in 1984 at Kamani auditorium, Delhi, *Pashu Gayatri* has so far had more than 175 shows in almost all major cultural centres of the country. *Amar Beej* has nearly had 100 performances. He also did *Dalpat Raja*. In 1992 Bhanu became critically ill. He had to leave Udaipur to get treatment in Mumbai. Meanwhile, one of his senior founder artists Roda Ram died in 1995. Fortunately, he recovered from his serious ailment and was once again back to his roots. He gathered lost threads of his organisation, weaving it once again in a well-knit group. New tribal youths joined the group—the show had to go on, it was unfolding with more gusto, dynamism and hope.

Pashu Gayatri is not a folk play; it is a modern work of theatre. The play is written by K.N. Panikkar. Bhanu's aim was to evolve a new language of theatre. *Pashu Gayatri* is a parable. 'I have retained the essence of the play while the superfluous elements have been removed. The play is an indictment of soul-destroying pursuit of wealth by man. It presents the image of a spiritually crippled modern man. The central thematic idea of the play revolves round a father who in his greed to grab treasure buried in the earth, does penance to please the snake god. He succeeds. The snake god accedes his prayers to take the buried treasure but on one condition. 'What is your most precious and dearest object?' asks the god. 'My son is dearest to me in the whole world,' he replies. The god says, 'Then sacrifice him to please the snakes that are guarding the treasure.' Blinded by greed, the father agrees to sacrifice his son. Here Panikkar displays a master-stroke and his deep insight into Hindu rituals. *Gayatri Mantra* is chanted while baptising a young Hindu to symbolise that he has become a member of an enlightened and pious clan. In a way it is the ritualistic initiation of a young man to the Hindu community. This is *Gayatri Mantra's* role of spiritual transformation. Here the father uses *Gayatri* for an object which is most inhuman and devilish. He uses it to transform his son into a cow so that he can sacrifice him. The boy turns into an animal. As an animal he confronts his adopted father who has no son and wants one to perform his last rites so that his soul can go to Heaven and he may achieve final salvation. The boy-turned-cow also confronts the butcher and his kind-hearted young daughter.

What fascinated Bhanu was the fable like moral power of the written script which has universal relevance. He discussed the play with his group of Gavari performers. Bhanu comments, 'When Panikkar was narrating this play to me I could see that this kind of play was impossible to realise [*sic*] with urban actors who would never (be) convinced that by merely reciting mantras a boy could be transformed into a cow. At that time, I was not working with Bheels but I had watched Gavari from close quarters. I immediately saw the possibility of producing it with them, hoping that they would respond to it. It was the spirit of the play that was important to me and not the script written by the playwright in its entirety. So it was very natural to experiment with the community to bring their culture and ethos into the theatre. I experimented with *Pashu Gayatri* and the result was amazing.'

In fact, using old forms with new content was initially started by the Indian People's Theatre Association. In this context Mulk Raj Anand's comment deserves special attention: 'I have had occasion to see how the groups of Indian People's Theatre Association in Andhra have rescued this form from the ignorant, who practised it as a formula and how, by composing new ballads with fresh social content, they have combined with the ... old form a new urgency of conscience, without diminishing any of the gaiety and joy which is inherent in the form itself.'[4]

This trend of discovering traditional, folk and tribal forms initiated by IPTA was reinforced by the Sangeet Natak Akademi scheme for young theatre directors with highly encouraging results in the early stages. But gradually the trend degenerated into revivalism with eyes closed to contemporary sensibilities. Some directors used these traditional elements to embellish their productions and to transform these works as an export commodity.

Bhanu has a different approach. He is a modern director with progressive vision. He believes in the collective character of art. He is

4. *The Indian Theatre* by Mulk Raj Anand, P 29

not disdainful of tribal rituals and their surrender to nature but defines these ancient rituals in the final analysis as man's innate desire to control nature and discover the element of causalty in natural phenomenon and in the development of social laws. For him both content and form are intrinsic elements in a work of art. In his theatrical experiments he seeks to achieve dialectical unity between these vital aspects of art. This is what makes Bhanu a highly creative and distinct director among his contemporaries. He is bold and ready to take risk, discover new possibilities and a new theatre language.

In dealing with *Pashu Gayatri* in Gavari style with his Bheel tribe, the elements Bhanu has incorporated into the narrative structure include Budhiya in green-and-white shorts. Holding a *chimta* (pincers) in one hand and a sword in the other, the brass beats tinkle while Budhiya dances, displaying full tribal energy. There is another powerful image, the image of the goddess Amba – a very important mythological character in Gavari – riding on the back of a lion. Her entry and her dance movements are charged with great power and energy. Amba is said to be one of the wives of Shiva. There entries are accompanied by musical instruments—*dhol* (drum), *madal* (brass plate), *manjeera* (cymbals) and the blowing of the conch. Then the snake god is worshipped, followed by the entry of another important character from Gavari called Kudkudiya, dressed in a red costume. Dramatic dialogues ensue between Budhiya and Kudkudiya. Kudkudiya prostrates before Budhiya. There is brief recitation, a kind of mantra used to transform the son into a cow. Intensely motivated movements, perfectly orchestrated with music and choreography, create a heart-rending atmosphere with the note '*Jhoothi Rey Kaya, Jhoothi Rey Maya*'. Bhopa, the conscience of the community, is present here to watch this ghastly act of a man to quench his greed.

Using the Gavari style, there is a large circle on the stage around which action takes place. In the most momentous and critical moment in the life of the son and the father, Budhiya goes into a trance, the sound of musical instruments acquire greater insistence and the choreography becomes vigorous. The mask is there, the speech pattern deserves special attention for its dramatic quality.

The most expressive elements in the production are music, choreography, lighting and costumes. There is minimal use of dialogues. The whole production creates a kind of symphony leaving the audience spellbound with vibrant undercurrents conveying the dilemma of spiritually crippled contemporary humanity which cuts across the boundaries of time and space.

A new language for Indian theatre is evolved. It is a live theatre with a distinct Indian colour, which breathes fresh air into the art form. Unfortunately, a few of our critics and leading theatre practitioners have viewed this experiment in a superficial manner, without dissecting the content and form of the play. Most of them do not know about the Bheel theatre form of Gavari, its dramatic elements and enduring appeal. They have preconceived notions of folk theatre. Rajendar Nath, eminent theatre director, writes on *Pashu Gayatri:* 'Take Bhanu Bharti's *Pashu Gayatri* which had the vigour of a folk play but remained at the folk level without really adding any contemporary dimension to the total experience.'[5]

Director Bhanu Bharti's comment on his use of this folk form in this context is as follows: 'Gavari, the community theatre of the Bheels in Mewar (Rajasthan), has always fascinated me. I see immense possibilities in the form, particularly because of its musical strain. The performance, as I have evolved it, is therefore conducted and regulated by the music. This provides an amazing force and flexibility to the entire production. After the present experiment I am absolutely confident that any theme, howsoever, "modern", can be tackled effectively in this form. More than his productions, the plays of Panikkar have interested me. This beautiful, poetic allegory is excellent material for any language. I have attempted to produce the work of a modern playwright in the Gavari form, with the original tribal players who are performing for the first time outside their milieu, minus the usual forty days of the long rituals which go with it. Achieving a secular, artistic performance outside the codes of strong religious beliefs and rituals has been extremely difficult but very exciting.'

5. Special issue *Traditional Idiom in Contemporary Theatre* (Sangeet Natak Akademi numbers 77-78) P 27

The playwright, Kavalam Narayan Panikkar – author of *Pashu Gayatri* – had witnessed Bhanu's version of *Pashu Gayatri* in Mewari. A leading Indian theatre personality and poet, Panikkar comments on *Pashu Gayatri* in an interview with the author.

'It is generally believed that in a translation, the spirit of the original is lost but in this type of experiment the translation or the translated version can work as a recreation of the original in the changed context. While the translator keeps pace with the original, the performance text itself is a re-creation of the original written text. The creativity of the director also plays an important role in extending the original thought process. Though some people criticised Bhanu's denouncement part, I don't know what exactly they meant. What I meant was that the gem of a boy is ultimately lost in the multitude and even his so-called kith and kin are not able to recognise him. He has even lost his father and has become a depersonalised character. (The play) is full of poetry and imagery. There is a moment in the play when the daughter of the butcher and the boy transcend their positions (mundane) and the conversation between them reflects a highly poetic and philosophical level. Until this point the boy never speaks except for some sounds and in my original version the name of the girl is Aringol, one who has attained wisdom. These are elements which make you imagine beyond the written text.

'The boy represents no one other than the Indian youth sold out. A coir with a knot and the coir rope in the original are symbols of the father's greed and the sensitivity of the butcher's daughter. Realisation comes to the father who feels the sense of loss—he reaches to the people who dance in ecstasy.

'Bhanu has done well in his production in Mewari of *Pashu Gayatri* because he maintained the simplicity by making the play agreeable to the Bheel artist to interact. The music too, positively reflects the tribal qualities of simplicity and the touch of liveliness that kept the play moving and interesting. I don't know what was lost in the subtle literary aspects of the original.'

Amar Beej: with a Bheel cast

One of his ladmark productions with tribals is *Amar Beej*. Inspired by Bheel mythology, Bhanu has reworked on it with a view to providing it with a contemporary ring.

He has used the elements of Gavari sparingly and creatively. The chorus with Gavari music score rendered with soulful voices that impart a haunting quality to the production, conveys the basic idea. The mythological characters like Amba and Shiva are endowed with metaphoric meaning. Amba symbolises goddess nature that sustains universe; it is a life giving force. There is Shiva who beats his *damru* and its *naad* – the loud musical sound – is the creator of nature and man and a symbol of primordial force. The interaction between Shiva and Amba symbolises the union between primeval male and female before the creation of the world.

On the surface of the play there is a woodcutter who uses his axe to fell a tree. On the first strike of the axe water emerges from the tree in torrents. The woodcutter does not stop and at the second strike of the axe flows milk and in the subsequent strikes blood gushes out—gradually spreading and rapidly drowning the vast expanse of earth. The whole cosmos appears to be filled with blood.

The basic thrust of the production is an urgent call to stop reckless exploitation of nature by man. If humanity is to survive there should be peaceful co-existence between man and nature.

Amar Beej is a multi-layered work of art, which never assumes a preachy tone. Bhanu is known for his highly innovative use of a piece of wood and fabric. Here he has used a huge piece of cloth held by human performers, creating the illusion of flowing water followed by a vast sea of milk and then the blood that floods almost the entire cosmos. This kind of illusionary effect is rarely seen on the Indian stage.

The powerful music is rendered by the chorus. Bhanu introduced female singers from the Bheel tribe for the first time on stage. The rhythmic and vivid dance movements and the mass scenes are not meant to simply dazzle the audience; they richly contribute to the expression of the basic thematic concern about endangered ecology and the preservation of nature and natural wealth for the survival of future generations.

Amar Beej was premiered in Udaipur and had fifteen shows in Delhi. A critique of Bhanu's other experimental pieces with his Bheel cast follow in the next few chapters.

Kaal Katha: the Bheel suffering

.... And their meaning is the inspiration of ancient working people to lighten their toil, increase its productiveness, to arm by the power of works, by the device of 'exorcism' and 'incantation' to gain an influence over the elemental phenomena of nature, which are hostile to men.... Their God is also not an abstract category, but a real personage, armed with some implements of labour, master of some trade, ambitious, vengeful, envious and hostile like men ... God was the artistic generalization of the achievements of labour and the 'religious' thought of the toiling masses should be placed in quotation marks, since it represented a purely artistic creativeness.

—Maxim Gorky

In late 1980s, Bhanu Bharti was engaged in research on the Bheel rituals and their place in the Bheel social life. He discussed various myths associated with the ritualistic practice of these tribal people, deliberately kept away by the ruling class from formal education and social transformation taking place in the rest of the country. Bhanu, the keen observer that he is, made an objective study of the debasing impact of famine on Bheel society and their rituals to ward off evil which they believe causes famine. Bheels are marginal farmers, settled in remote hilly regions with little facilities for irrigation. Bhanu weaved a tale out of this man-made tragedy and transformed it with a fine dramatic piece after interacting with his Bheel performers. The result was a play which he called *Kaal Katha*. It reflects the stark reality in the lives of the impoverished and superstitious Bheels. The play also tries to project that even in the midst of vast devastation and human misery, the noble instinct of man survives and redeems the baseness of a cruel society.

Written in Mewari, *Kaal Katha* is probably the first significant play written in the Hindi region. Of course, we know about *Nabanna* in Bengali which captures the suffering of people dying of starvation on the streets of Kolkata during the infamous famine of 1943. Written by Bijon Bhatttacharya and directed by Shambu Mitra in collaboration with the playwright for the Indian People's Theatre Association, it marked the beginning of a new theatre movement in Bengal.

Nabanna captures a vast landscape of human misery at the time of harrowing famine juxtaposing with the hated affluent class and hoarders trading in human suffering. Structurally, it is episodic. Bhanu's *Kaal Katha* explores an innocent young woman's struggle to escape from being sacrificed to propitiate angry gods who are believed to have caused widespread devastation. The ordeal of the young woman, the famine and people unable to get rid of the tentacles of superstition, form the basic structure of the narrative, creating a drama which is intricate. The underlying philosophy seeks to harmonise humanity and nature.

Gauri is the protagonist of the play. There is all-round intense deprivation caused by drought. The ambience is tribal. At a meeting of the community the cause of drought is diagnosed by the priest who also declares its solution. The gods are angry. To escape from their fury, a virgin girl should be sacrificed whose pure blood can please the gods and only then will they free the tribal society from the scourge of famine. Gauri, an innocent virgin tribal girl is chosen for sacrifice by the priest and community. Here the script acquires the tragic dimension of Iphigenia, the central character of *Iphigenia in Autis* by Euripides (484-406 BC) but unlike Iphigenia Gauri does not surrender to the superstitious masses. She is bold, intelligent, sharp and above all, she loves life. Sensing what is in store for her in the midst of rituals and celebrations, she escapes wandering through forests. She has an encounter with an agent of the flesh trade who gets hold of her and sells her at an auction at a very high price to an old man. Happy with his purchase, the old man and Gauri pass through a dense forest. She befriends the old man, winning his trust, manages to kill him with a heavy stone and becomes free once more. Then she encounters an aggressive lion, moving menacingly towards Gauri. In a desperate bid to protect herself, she jumps and sits on the back of the lion. Taken aback by the courage and alacrity of a girl the lion moves on with Gauri on his back. Here enters a dreaded dacoit Goma, a staunch worshipper of Durga. He faints to see the image of a 'goddess' on the back of a lion. Gauri takes this opportunity to put on his clothes and disguised as Goma, commands his gang to plunder the granaries and stores of rich farmers and those controlling the black market.

Though her people bay for her blood and look for her frantically from place to place, Gauri is moved to see their plight when they dye of starvation. She watches the debasement of humanity caused by the famine with a heavy heart. There are images of mothers eating the flesh of their own children. Possessed with an earnest desire to alleviate the suffering of the starving people she orders her men to distribute the looted grain among the tribal people who are puzzled to discover the change of heart of their 'leader' but they obey her grudgingly.

The climactic scene is significant in terms of dramatic richness and the deeply philosophical overtones of the play. Overwhelmed to see the generosity of the 'dacoit' Goma, the tribal people declare 'him' their tribal head in a ritualistic ceremony. In a moment of ecstasy Gauri who has all along been in the guise of Goma, discloses her real identity. Far from being happy to see their own Gauri in their midst and expressing their sincere gratitude for all that she did to provide them with grain during the days of draught, they become furious, expressing their wish to sacrifice her and please the gods with her blood. Gauri does not resist; she remains standing defenceless. But before the crowd gets hold of her emerges the real dacoit Goma in the guise of a woman following Gauri all along, challenging Gauri's captors. Watching the real dreaded dacoit the tribals beat a hasty retreat.

The denouement, which shows the masses as an ungrateful, stubborn lot, appears to be closer to the treatment of the masses as the perpetrators of the municipal corruption opposing a man of truth in *An Enemy of the People* by Henrik Ibsen (1828-1906).

Bhanu has blended the elements of Gavari with the modernistic theatrical techniques. In *Pashu Gayatri* Bhanu has used more elements from Gavari but in *Kaal Katha* he has used these elements for the tribal theatre form rather sparingly. The description of collecting honey from the jungle in the play is taken from an interesting episode in Gavari theatre. The various myths, customs and tribal traditions are drawn from Bheel tribal forms. These elements do not appear to be superimposed but are an integral part of the narrative.

The use of masks is inspired by Gavari. In the tribal tradition these masks are made of wood. In Bhanu's production these are made of *papier mâché*. The costumes are inspired by Gavari tradition but they are designed with a sophisticated touch.

Music drawn from the Bheel rituals and Gavari theatre forms an important element of *Kaal Katha*. The review of the production at Kamani auditorium, New Delhi in 1988 by the author as published in the *Indian Express* is as follows: 'Music is treated as one of the main expressive means, commenting at places, summarising the significance of the action and enriching the mood which ranges from grotesque to fearful and from pathetic to heroic'.

Tribal instruments like *madal, thaali* (bronze plate) and flutes are used to heighten dramatic intensity in situations like the rituals to offer human sacrifice to the angry gods. Since most of the action takes place in the remote hilly region surrounded by dense forest, mysterious forest music is created with human voices. Here Bhanu has achieved a rare artistic feat while capturing the myriad moods of the forest, ranging from the elegant to the cheerful. The presentation is rich in visual and aural appeal. The images such as Gauri riding a lion symbolises the powerful image of Durga. Kavita Nagpal wrote in the *Hindustan Times* in 1988: '. . . the drama (*Kaal Katha*) is almost a story of their lives (Bheel tribals) in their own words placed in theatrical reality via their own special life rhythms produced by nature's assault and man's insensitivity'.

The dramatic treatment of the script, the stage spectacles, movements and music together create a rare, gripping theatricality. The dénouement deserves a special mention. The ungrateful and obscurantist masses disappear from the scene. Gauri and Goma occupy the centre stage with an inspiring music as backdrop. They dance ecstatically with the whole forest joining them in the dance projected by suggestive sets designed on jute sprayed with colours, symbolising the harmony between man and nature. The sets were designed by eminent painter Shail Choyal based in Udaipur.

There are twenty-one characters in the play and all the performers were Bheel tribals—born actors and singers. The urban audience at the Kamani marvelled at the excellent performances of these tribals who adapted themselves to the modern stage technique. Dhakuri as Gauri and Khema as Goma, Mana as the priest and Deva as the lion create portrayals of their characters that are indelible.

Much later, while on a trip to the Bheel village at Udaipur to study Gavari theatre, the author met Dhakuri who continues to be associated with Bhanu. She has fond memories of her performance at various places in India and of the warm welcome she received from the audience.

Adaptation of a Japanese tale told by a scorched tree, *Katha Kahi Ek Jale Ped Ne* (1981) has two narrators representing the tree (*Courtesy: Bhanu Bharti*)

Scene from *Katha Kahi Ek Jale Ped Ne* where the painter foresees the doom of the monkey race (*Courtesy: Bhanu Bharti*)

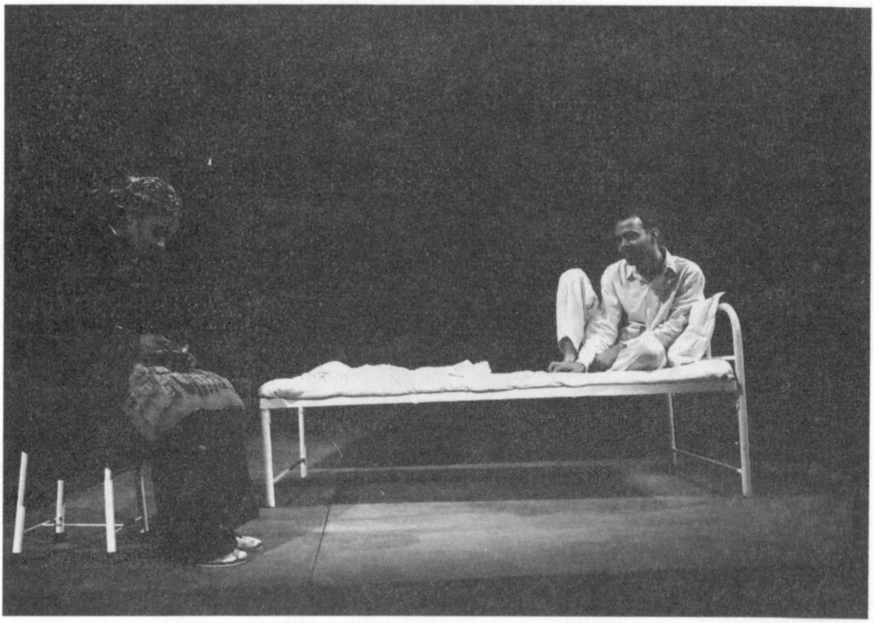

Lokendra Trivedi as the invalid and Meera Mishra as his wife in a modern Japanese play, *The Elephant* (1981) (*Courtesy: National School of Drama, Delhi*)

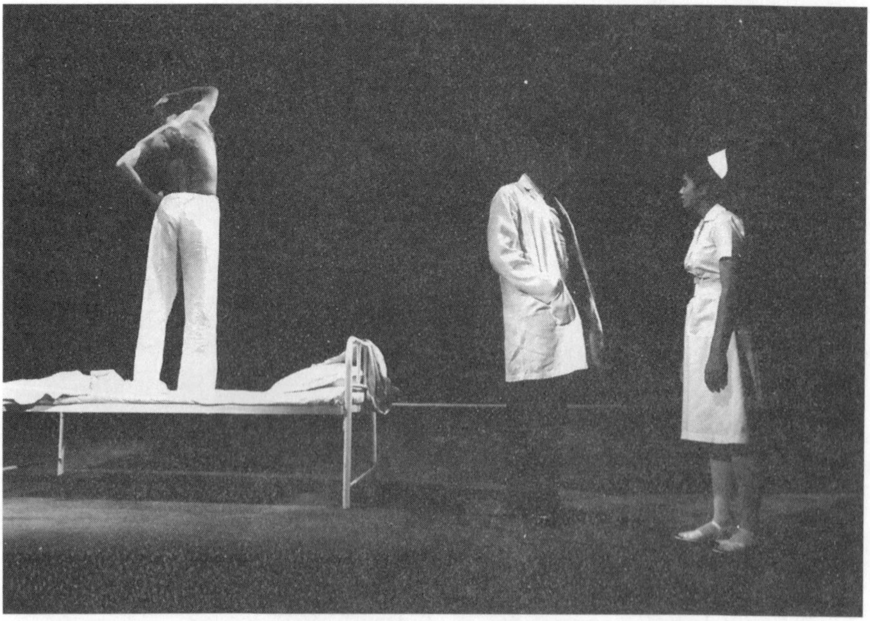

Deepa Sahi as nurse, Bharat Bhushan Suri as the doctor and Lokendra Trivedi as the invalid in *The Elephant* (1981) (*Courtesy: National School of Drama, Delhi*)

The Elephant (1981) with Lokendra Trivedi as the invalid (foreground) and Suresh Shetty as nephew (*Courtesy: National School of Drama, Delhi*)

Nephew (Suresh Shetty)and the nurse in *The Elephant* (1981) (*Courtesy: National School of Drama, Delhi*)

Nurse with a doll in *The Elephant* (1981)
(*Courtesy: National School of Drama, Delhi*)

Bhanu Bharti with the cast of *The Elephant* (1981)
(*Courtesy: National School of Drama, Delhi*)

Ek Sapne Ki Maut (1982)—an adaptation of Arthur Miller's *Death of a Salesman*. Lalit Behl as the salesman (*right*) and Sanjeeva Sahai as Charandas (*Courtesy: Shriram Centre*)

A scene from *Pashu Gayatri* (1984) with Bheel performers. An adaptation of K.N. Panikkar's Malayalam play, this uses tenets of Bheel rituals associated with their community theatre Gavari (*Courtesy: Sangeet Natak Akademi*)

Anang Desai, Seema Biswas (standing), Ravi Khaanwilkar and Raghuvir Yadav (sitting; foreground) in *Chandrama Singh urf Chamku* (1985) (*Courtesy: National School of Drama, Delhi*)

A scene from *Chandrama Singh urf Chamku* (1985) with Raghuvir Yadav as Chamku, Anang Desai as the landlord and Ravi Khaanwilkar as the chowkidar. Vallabh Vyas is the muscleman and Suresh Shetty – the son of the landlord (*Courtesy: National School of Drama, Delhi*)

A scene from the play *Chandrama Singh urf Chamku* (1985) in which Raghuvir Yadav plays Chandrama Singh (*Courtesy: National School of Drama, Delhi*)

A scene from *Chandrama Singh urf Chamku* (1985) with Nutan Surya and Surekha Sikri (*Courtesy: National School of Drama, Delhi*)

Raghuvir Yadav and others at the *thekka* (wine shop) in *Chandrama Singh urf Chamku* (1985) (*Courtesy: National School of Drama, Delhi*)

Raghuvir Yadav (left) and Vageesh Kumar Singh as the village priest in a scene from *Chandrama Singh urf Chamku* (1985) (*Courtesy: National School of Drama, Delhi*)

Uttara Baokar, Dev and Anang Desai at a nautanki performance in the play *Chandrama Singh urf Chamku* (1985) (*Courtesy: National School of Drama, Delhi*)

At a tea shop with villagers in the play *Chandrama Singh urf Chamku* (1985) (*Courtesy: National School of Drama, Delhi*)

Jitendra Shastri as Pururva in captivity in the play *Yum Gatha* (1990)
(*Courtesy: National School of Drama, Delhi*)

Indra and Pururva in *Yum Gatha* (1990)
(*Courtesy: National School of Drama, Delhi*)

Yum Gatha (1990) with Ballabh Vyas as Indra and Suresh Shetty as Vishavasu
(*Courtesy: National School of Drama, Delhi*)

Jitendra Shastri as Pururva, being executed in *Yum Gatha* (1990)
(*Courtesy: National School of Drama, Delhi*)

A dramatic moment in *Yum Gatha* (1990) with Himani Shivpuri as Urvashi along with Navratna and the priest at the sacrificial altar. (*Courtesy: National School of Drama, Delhi*)

Ravi Khaanwilkar in *Yum Gatha* (1990) with Jitendra Shastri as Pururva distributing heavenly fire among villagers (*Courtesy: National School of Drama, Delhi*)

Scene from *Amar Beej* (1991)—a play on environment issues with Bheel actors, based on a Bheel legend. (*Courtesy: Sangeet Natak Akademi*)

A Hindi translation of Chandrasekhar Kambar's Kannada play *Siri Sampige*, *Aks-Tamasha* (1996) has Mahendra Mewati as the Prince and Sapna Sand as the Mother Queen (*Courtesy: National School of Drama, Delhi*)

The Mother Queen played by Sapna Sand, with wise men in *Aks-Tamasha* (1996) (*Courtesy: National School of Drama, Delhi*)

The Prince (Mahendra Mewati) and his wife Shampa (Mandakini Goswami) in *Aks-Tamasha* (1996) (*Courtesy: National School of Drama, Delhi*)

Mahendra Mewati as the Prince and Mandakini Goswami as Shampa, wife of the Prince in *Aks-Tamasha* (1996) (*Courtesy: National School of Drama, Delhi*)

The Nagraj (Snake) in *Aks-Tamasha* (1996), played by Subrata Dutta as the divided half of the Prince (*Courtesy: National School of Drama, Delhi*)

Vijay Raj as Prince in *Aks-Tamasha* (1996) before dividing himself into two halves (*Courtesy: National School of Drama, Delhi*)

The Prince and his wife in *Aks-Tamasha* (1996)
(*Courtesy: National School of Drama, Delhi*)

Subrata Dutta as Nagraj in *Aks-Tamasha* (1996) (*Courtesy: National School of Drama, Delhi*)

Subrata Dutta as Nagraj and Mandakini Goswami as Shampa. Nagraj seducing the Prince's wife Shampa in *Aks-Tamasha* (1996) (*Courtesy: National School of Drama, Delhi*)

Court of the Mother Queen in *Aks-Tamasha* (1996) where the Prince charges his wife Shampa of adultery (*Courtesy: National School of Drama, Delhi*)

The Prince's wife Shampa with the child fathered by the Nagraj in *Aks-Tamasha* (1996) (*Courtesy: National School of Drama, Delhi*)

A poignant scene from *Aks-Tamasha* (1996) where Shampa proves her innocence in the adultery charge (*Courtesy: National School of Drama, Delhi*)

Abli-Jabli—the twins mirroring the main plot at an absurd level in *Aks-Tamasha* (1996). Parag Sarmah plays Abli while Sameep Singh is Jabli (*Courtesy: National School of Drama, Delhi*)

Sindhu Mishra in *Naachni* (1998)—a play expressing a folk dancer's moments of agony and ecstasy (*Coutesy: Bhanu Bharti*)

Scene from *Naachni* with Sindhu Mishra depicting the various shades of emotions of an oppressed artiste (*Coutesy: Bhanu Bharti*)

Aks-Tamasha: milestone in contemporary Indian theatre

The object of all art is to appeal not only to the mind and feelings, but to the imagination, to arouse the imagination and set it working in a new, unexpected direction, that it would never have come to of its own accord.

—Georgia Tovstonogov

In the context of fast changing times and space, I do not find that any explored form can define complexities. A successful experiment becomes a cliché to me. I will move to something still unexplored.

—Bhanu Bharti

A theatrical masterpiece, *Aks-Tamasha* provides a profound insight into the inner conflict of man, into the perpetual conflict between reality and illusion and the dialectical antagonism between self and the other self. The production also dissects the conflict of Ardhanareeshwar symbolised in the 'person' of Lord Shiva with its connotation of the tormented modern man. Such a philosophically intense play needs a highly intricate theatrical treatment, which is different from the conventional style of presentation.

A Hindi translation of eminent Kannada poet and playwright Chandrasekhar Kambar's play *Siri Sampige* by Ram Gopal Bajaj, *Aks-Tamasha* in the original format is in Yakshgana style. Since Bhanu Bharti is no expert in Yakshgana, he faced a formidable challenge in the choice of an appropriate style of presentation when he was directing the Hindi version for NSD. He read this play several times and held several readings with his actors. He was impressed with the complexities, multiple levels and intricacies of the play.

On the surface, there is a mythological aura; the invocation to Lord Shiva and the general ambience reinforce that aura. A kingdom is ruled by a queen after her husband's, the king's death. She rules with the advice of the elders and the wise. There is an oracle and God—controlling the destiny of man. The setting tends to be quite similar to that of Greek tragedy.

The queen has a son. She now wants to get the prince married, and to hand over the reins of the kingdom to him. She is preoccupied with the prophecy of the oracle which says if the prince spots his reflection either on a mirror or water, his life would be in danger. However, the search for a suitable match for the prince continues, frantically. In quest of a perfect queen, the prince has rejected all prospective brides. One day in a highly reflective mood and lost in a fantasy world he watches the sculpture of the lamp stand on the wall come alive in the form of an exquisitely beautiful girl and invite him to make love to her. In an ecstatic mood the prince follows her and, in a mysterious way, feels that her image has entered his soul. Obsessed with an ominous perception about this image within him, he orders his body to be ripped apart into two lengthwise, each part be preserved in a separate pot, subsequently buried among flowers and be opened after a week.

Struck by terror, the order of the prince is carried out. When the pots are opened a dreadful snake emerges from one pot and disppears and, from the other, comes out the prince himself. This happens contrary to the wish of the prince—who wanted the beautiful woman to emerge from one of the pots so that he could finally marry her.

This episode puts the prince in a feverish state of mind; he continues to look for the creature that came out from one of the pots. Meanwhile, his mother forcefully gets him married to princess Shampa. The prince disdainfully refuses to accept her as his wife and continues to wander in the forests during night, leaving his sex-starved wife alone in the palace.

Wandering through the forest, he catches his reflection in the water. What he perceives is strange and horrible.

Meanwhile, infatuated by the sensuous beauty of the sex-starved wife of the prince, a snake enters her room. Unable to control herself, Shampa surrenders to the sexual advances of the snake. In due course she becomes pregnant and delivers a male child. Whenever the snake enters the palace, he comes in the guise of the prince. The entire royal household is celebrating the pregnancy of Shampa but the prince charges her with adultery and the matter is referred to the elders for justice. The prince feels his wife has brought dishonour to the royal family and he must defend the reputation of the family even at the cost of his own life. He inflicts mortal wounds on the snake; gazes deep into his eyes and finds the reflection of his own body and soul. The prince declares that the child born to Shampa is his own child because the snake is his other self, his twin. With these words the prince takes his last breath.

The play has a tragic climactic end. Finally, the prince perceives his own reflection in the eyes of the snake he has killed in a duel and discovers his other self.

What makes the play highly complicated is the creation of two characters—Abli and Jabli. On the surface they appear to be comic characters to provide relief. They are twins and completely identical, enacting actions similar to what the Prince performs. Like the prince, who is engaged in a battle with the snake which emerges out of his half-severed part, the twins too get engaged in fierce fighting between themselves. They are not comic characters but rather tragic and grotesque—capturing the dangerous and intense hatred taking birth within man who is in perpetual conflict with his other self.

A play of this complexity demands a directorial approach which ventures beyond the conventional style of presentation. Similarly, a stylised format may not bring the philosophical richness of the play to the fore. Bhanu writes in his note: 'I do not know why Kambar chose to write the play in the traditional Yakshagana form of theatre in Karnataka. I have not seen it performed in that style, and I am no authority on Yakshagana but I feel that any traditional theatre form in its stylistic fixation will create serious problems at the level of thematic communicability of the play. Because of this, I had to struggle hard to liberate the play from its given form and re-create it, along with my actors and musicians in a form which would bring forth the multiple and complex treatment of the subject effectively for the modern theatre audience, outside the Karnataka milieu.

'In doing so, I have been careful not to disturb the original theatrical directness and apparent simplicity of the play. I have tried to achieve that through the blending of ritualistic and folk theatre elements with other theatrical tools from contemporary theatre. I have also taken care not to tamper the text in the process. At the most what I have done is to combine a few scenes and to redistribute the text among the characters. I am glad that in doing so, I have met with complete agreement of my playwright.'

Bhanu's conception of the production of *Aks-Tamasha,* which was presented at Shri Ram Centre, New Delhi on 19 October 1996 is remarkable for its innovation of the theatrical language. In collaboration with his actors and music composer Ravi Nagar he had created a complex piece of theatrical art rich in ideas and in the music of words, rhythms and colours.

The sets were designed by the director himself. If the style of presentation is a synthesis of a variety of styles, the sets are distinctively original. Fabric is an essential element of Bhanu's artistic credo. They add a variety of colours and moods to the production but what is unique in this production is that at times the sets become characters and, at other times they reflect the most tense moments in the life of the characters and the turmoil within their inner worlds in an almost abstract form, which is highly imaginative, subtle and expressive. Huge draperies are hung upstage against the wall. There is a raised platform for the entry and exit of performers. The draperies are also used as a screen to depict shadow puppets, revealing such intensely emotional and erotic moments as the union between a passionate snake and a sexually starved, young and neglected wife of a prince. These shadows of a man and woman are a rare manifestation of eroticism. These draperies are also used to project the scene where the prince is ripped from his head downwards into two parts.

On the centerstage there is large circle which gives the impression of a *vedi* (alter); this is the area where the main dramatic action takes place—in a style similar to the performance of *yajna*. Around this circle on a raised area members of the chorus occupy their place on one side. On this *vedi* four characters, who claim to be twins, are sacrificed. Except a small stool there is no other property used in the production. Most male characters wear specially designed masks in two different colours to reflect the inner dialectic that exists in man. The costumes draped by Kriti V. Sharma capture the royal grandeur. The music, on the one hand, conducts the play and on the other, acquires a provocative tone to impart vitality and strong motivation to the performers.

Bhanu has used pauses and silences with remarkable dramatic effect imparting greater depth and emotional power to the production. The whole production is a symphony that stirs the human soul. There is hardly any fade-out. The action follows in a seamless manner with the audience irresistibly drawn to an intense dramatic action on the stage.

Here it will be interesting to refer to Girish Karnad's *Nagamandala*. On the surface both *Aks-Tamasha* and *Nagamandala* tell the story of the archetypal loveless woman, a victim of her husband's cold indifference and in both plays the two women discover their sexual fulfillment in a snake. In both, the husbands charge their wives with adultery and in both the women are subjected to a chastity test by facing the highly poisonous cobra and the lover cobras oblige these women by sparing their lives. The public adores these women and raise them to the pedestal of a 'devi' or a deity.

Both Kambar and Karnad are Kannada playwrights. Kambar wrote *Aks-Tamasha* in 1980 and Karnad created *Nagamandala* in 1988. *Nagamandala* has a sub-plot in which a son suddenly leaves his blind mother and in the search of a girl. The relationship of the sub-plot with the main plot is difficult to discern. In the main plot of *Nagamandala*, Rani is the protagonist. In Kambar's play Shampa is the protagonist.

The story of Abli and Jabli could be described as a sub-plot which has dialectical relationship with the main plot. The relationship is clear and unambiguous. Karnad's Rani is apologetic and is initially ignorant about the real identity of the serpent which comes to her bed in the guise of her husband. However, in *Aks-Tamasha* Shampa knows the real identity of the snake from her first encounter with it and she faces her husband boldly when he accuses her of adultery.

Kambar's play in its Hindi version as *Aks-Tamasha* is of epic dimensions and resonates with lyricism, lending to its universal appeal.

Bhanu is highly impressed with Kambar's plays. 'His writing is very dense and poetic; his plays have poetic density which I don't find in many contemporary playwrights, including Girish Karnad.'

The Elephant: a sensitive work

It goes without saying that this is something very close to the performance of old Japanese itinerant entertainers and story tellers. Betsuyaku's image of the post-war period is bound up with the small theatrical acts performed on burned out streets of Hiroshima and it is from there that the play derives its peculiar theatrical power.

—Bhanu Bharti

Bhanu Bharti during his stay in Japan for one-and-a-half years studied Japanese classical theatre forms. Before he could start his main study, he had to join classes of Japanese language. A sensitive and keen observer of life and society, he studied the latest trends in Japanese literature – especially theatre – both classical and contemporary. Once in his classroom he said that yet another World War is inevitable. Both the students and teacher were shocked to hear his statement. Unable to grasp the reason behind the reaction of the class to his casual remark, he gradually realised how the trauma of mass devastation of human life and society caused by the nuclear bomb dropped by the USA on Nagasaki and Hiroshima had deeply scarred the psyche of young Japanese people. He visited the sites where the nuclear bombs were dropped. The exhibitions of the dreadful images of the victims, the scenes of mass murder, the rocky surfaces which had indelible impressions of human bodies which fell on them and were burnt to death by the bomb and the twisted remains of heavy iron lockers—all this disturbed Bhanu deeply.

He then realised the folly of his remark about another World War. The fate of the survivors was dreadful. Affected by radiation they met a slow and painful death, their bodies twisting to horrible forms.

Bhanu observed that young men whose parents were victims of this ghastly crime against humanity preferred not to marry as they believed they were carriers of infected genes. The rescue workers, hospital doctors and nurses also became victims of radiation in due course.

Once Bhanu read a play written by absurdist playwright Betsuyaku Minoru in an avant garde Japanese magazine. He was a little-known playwright then. But his play *The Elephant* deeply impressed Bhanu. The play captures the aftermath of nuclear bombing on human society, the relationship between men and the absurdity of the human situation in a dreadful world infected by radiation. The play demanded a totally unconventional style of acting, presentation and interpretation of the spectacle of human suffering and destruction.

When Bhanu returned to India after successfully completing his study, he brought the magazine back with him and began his search of a talented cast for this play. He got the opportunity when the then director of the National School of Drama, the late B.M. Shah invited him to do a play with the fellows of the advance study course of NSD.

The play was translated into Hindi by V.K. Sharma. The protagonist of the play is an invalid and a survivor of the nuclear bombing of Hiroshima. He carries festering scars from the radiation. His body is disfigured. He has a carbuncle on his back. All these deformities and pain increase with each passing day and ultimately bring his death. This process of dehumanisation has robbed him of the sense of human dignity. Standing by the crossroads, he displays his deformities to anxious onlookers who give him some alms. A stage comes when his disease becomes severe; he is hospitalised, waiting for his slow death.

The invalid experiences many nightmarish visions and battles with his feverish mind on the death bed. He wants to escape from the hospital, desperate to demonstrate his highly deformed and dreadful body to curious onlookers. He fantasises a town in which he can earn his bread by showing his fast decaying body and his blisters. He also imagines that in case the spectators are not impressed, he would cut his body and splatter it all over. His wish is not to die an inevitable death on the hospital bed in his sleep.

❧

In a world of mass death and the inevitability of death of radiation-infected humanity, the society becomes dehumanised, grotesque. Human relations lose their meaning. This is aptly reflected through the character of the wife of the invalid. She comes to visit her husband in the hospital but does not meet or talk to him, as he lies isolated in a single room. The significance and nuances of their relationship are lost for ever. During her stay in the hospital ward, the wife continues to eat. Similarly, the doctor has lost interest in his patient who is neither dead nor alive!

Bhanu writes his note on the play as follows:

'Sufferers of the atomic bomb explosion and victims of cadmium-polluted water supplies, burdened with deformities of their flesh are forced today to live as outcasts—(made so) by the contemptuous, frightened glances of people around them. The invalid's keloid—like the brands carved into the bodies of criminals in ancient Greece, or like the rose-shaped bruise set to form on the skin of the chosen in medieval Christian society—functions as a kind of stigma. His keloid is proof for all to see that he belongs to a small group alien to normal social order and both evil and sacrosanct, it compels him towards a cognizance of theatrical elements at the very centre of his life.'

As Bhanu observes, the play structurally derives from Japan's itinerant entertainers and story-tellers. The protagonist often uses this mode to relate ghastly accounts of the victims of the nuclear explosion and he repeats the same story-telling technique through his nightmarish visions while he is confined to a hospital bed. Bhanu adds, 'Betsuyaku's image of the post-war period is bound up with the small theatrical acts performed on burnt down streets of Hiroshima and it is from there that the play derives its peculiar theatrical power'.

This is a play which is new both in content and form—for the audience as well as the performers. The play does not use presentation technique. It has two spaces – mental and physical – and these spaces are fluid and vague. The characters are extremely real and yet they look fictitious like the characters of absurd theatre. Though the play deals with the most ghastly and barbaric act committed by a 'super power', presenting the most tragic spectacle of mass murder in recent history and its dreadful after-effects, the play does not resort to sloppy sentimentalism. There is tragedy in the comic and the comic in tragedy. The invalid is suffering from deformity and he is grotesque and yet comical. The nephew finds this absurdity at the deepest level and is incapable of describing; yet he is condemned to communicate. The world in which the characters inhabit is mechanical as well as comical. It is devoid of all possibilities of life; it virtually denies life and is a buffer zone between life and death.

Bhanu comments: 'Among all the plays I have directed, *The Elephant* stands out as far as its conceptualisation is concerned. Artistically valid theatre (was created) out of a complex, intricate, multi-layered, poetic and dialectical plot....'

The play was presented at AIFACS in 1981. The sets were austere. There is poetic intensity and lyricism in the play. The director has created metaphorical imagery to reflect the inherent philosophic overtones of the play. The recorded instrumental music was used with remarkable subtlety. The light design by R.K. Dhingra contributed to create an atmosphere that enabled the performers to reveal their inner world. This is a work of theatrical art that would give a direction to the Hindi theatre movement. Bhanu has worked very hard to bring out the best in his cast and present a most complex play for which they had no previous experience. Lokendra Trivedi in the challenging role of the invalid, Suresh Shetty as the nephew, Meera as the wife of the invalid patient, Deepa Sahi as nurse and Bharat Bhushan Suri as the doctor gave a brilliant account of themselves. Most performers of this play are now well-known names in the world of theatre and films.

In the words of Sarveshwar Dayal Saxena, poet, playwright and critic, 'Those who have seen this production would continue to remember this for its images of Japanese life and poetic lyricism'. This is a dark and nightmarish world in which the inhabitants and the medical staff are both progressively decaying, moving painfully towards inevitable death. They are even denied natural death; they are terrified of dying in sleep, fantasising a world where they breathe freely and die a natural death. The audience watches this ghastly spectacle of human misery with bated breath.

As far as the title of the play *The Elephant* is concerned there is hardly any reference to an elephant. Bhanu suggests the elephant to be 'a sacred symbol of Buddhism … (which) stands for human freedom to be preserved, regardless of mass murders committed in concentration camps or by the atomic bombs. (This) in itself explains the title well enough.'

Recounting his experience of essaying the role of the invalid, Lokendra Trivedi gives the following account:

'Bhanu Sir was not satisfied with my work. My portrayal of the invalid in the advance stage of deformity with his flesh rotting tended to be superficial and external. The scene between me and Suresh Shetty who was playing the role of the invalid's nephew was repeatedly rehearsed. But there was little improvement in the quality of performance. With instructions from Bhanu Sir the rehearsal was postponed for three days. We reassembled and the rehearsal began. My acting style continued to be superficial. Bhanu Sir took out his belt and hit me hard, shouting, "Do you feel the pain now? Your character is feeling both physical and inner pain, internalise it and then express it." This incident brought about a transformation in my approach to the character of the invalid. Today, after nearly three decades when I reflect on my performance of the invalid, I feel that I did justice to this highly challenging role which followed no conventional method.

'When the show was over, Naseeruddin Shah came up on to the stage, embraced me and said, "This is a great performance. After *The Lesson* (in that play Naseer played the role of the professor), *The Elephant* is another masterpiece by Bhanu."

'Since then I have become a great admirer of Bhanu Sir. He is a theatre director with originality … in quest of perfection in all aspects of theatrical art. I watched him with keen interest while he was adapting in Hindi the celebrated story *'The True Story of Ah Q'* by Lu Hsun for students of NSD. I was then a NSD repertory actor. He is the director who goes into details of theatrical arts, devoting himself totally. Later, when he was doing Doodhnath Singh's *Yum Gatha* for NSD repertory, I was associated with the production and played the role of Vibhavak.' In *The Elephant* Bhanu evolved a new style and a new genre – these are the characteristics of a pioneer.

The play brings home with shocking awareness the fact that nuclear bomb explosion caused mass murders and the survivors and the rescue and the health workers met with a most grotesque, painful death, physically decaying and rotting, presenting a dreadful spectacle of human misery. The humanity must condemn those who perpetuate such heinous and brutal crimes against masses and raise a powerful voice against neo-colonialism and its design to maim and kill innocent people.

Yum Gatha: a complex creative work

"The way in which the implicity of the Vedic lyrics and the atmosphere of brilliance has been recreated, the use of rhetoric in their repetitions is unforgettable. I was happy to see the manner in which Dhoodhnath Singh has used the chorus and inspiring chants as in Greek tragedy

—Prof. Namvar Singh

Yum Gatha is one of the most daring innovations in the history of modern Indian theatre. In this experimental theatrical piece Bhanu sought to synthesise various theatrical genres like Western theatre, Indian folk theatre, Brechtian epic theatre and Greek tragic theatre—creating a new theatre form at once Indian and universal in appeal. It has music, dramatic dialogue, poetry, choreography and two antagonistic forces at war with one another and passionate love which are woven into the basic structure of the script. In the words of Romesh Chander, a veteran theatre critic, 'Bhanu Bharti's production is a beautiful synthesis of our classical theatre, the epic style a la Brecht and folk theatre without joining the folk bandwagon.'

The play was staged by NSD's Repertory Company at Meghdoot's open-air theatre in New Delhi in 1990 with great expectations to welcome a new play in Hindi by a progressive poet and scholar who spent years in research culminating in a serious work of drama with a remarkable contemporary ring.

The play explores the myth of Pururva and Urvashi's romance against the background of Vedic ritualistic civilisation. This myth has been eulogised by our great poets like Kalidasa, Dinkar and Rabindra Nath Tagore. What insight and new interpretation Doodhnath Singh imparts to this story is his original contribution which enriches Hindi dramaturgy, giving it a new dimension.

In an interview the playwright gave to Shamsul Islam in 1990, he explains that he wanted to liquidate the myth about the golden age of Vedic culture by Hindutva elements to highlight the Brahminical exploitative system. He adds there were two classes—the ruling and the exploited. The suppressed classes in the leadership of Pururva and his non-Aryan Brahmin Guru Vasistha waged a violent struggle against the ruling classes, which consisted of Indra, the priets, the saints, the kings and the gandharvas. Pururva succeeded in liberating Urvashi from the decadent court of Lord Indra, brought Agni (Fire) from there and distributed to the dispossessed. Doodhnath Singh asserts that this struggle was essentially a class struggle and it continues even today. In the words of the playwright, 'It is because of this that the Rig Veda describes Pururva as the 'friend of death' and the Brahminical texts call him '*Yajna* destroyer' and mad ('*Nashta-Sangyah*').

In this way, *Yum Gatha* deals with the Rig Veda's mythical world and expresses from within the so-called 'Holy Murder' by the ruling classes of their opponents. This is the fundamental objective of this play in our contemporary world'.

Eminent scholar Namvar Singh describes *Yum Gatha* in these words, 'When one views this play which is primarily one of socio-political revolt, one discovers that the author has carried the deep and delicate love-episode of Pururva-Urvashi with complete dignity and command and yet it is full-blooded. This is the biggest danger for any artist ... and the biggest test.' (NSD Brouchure)

Doodhnath is probably the first playwright in Hindi who raised the character of Pururva to the height of a primal rebel. We have known

Spartacus as the primal rebel who fought with the exploited gladiators against the exploitative aristocracy of the Great Roman Empire. American novelist Howard Fast has immortalised Spartacus in his novel of the same title. Later, a Hollywood film gave Spartacus worldwide popularity. He was a staunch believer in struggle against oppression and has love for freedom. His story is a genuine tragedy. Spartacus was a fierce fighter against the enemies of humanity and also a passionate lover who loved a slave woman with all his heart. So is our Pururva, a great tragic hero and a primal rebel.

Pururva has another dimension to his character. He brings fire from Indra's capitivity and distributes it to the outcaste and oppressed and brings light and happiness to their lives, which were initially condemned to live in poverty, ignorance and perpetual bondage. We know about the Prometheus myth, as the one who brought fire from heaven for men on earth. Aeschylus (525 BC-456 BC) the Greek dramatist, wrote *Prometheus Bound* (460 BC). Goethe and Shelly wrote poems on his courage and deep concerns for man. Poet and playwright Dharmveer Bharati composed a poem on him. However, it is Doodhnath who discovered in Pururva a primal liberator who brought fire from heavenly control for humanity.

Before going through the printed version of *Yum Gatha* Bhanu had known Doodhnath Singh and his works. He was impressed with his *Yum Gatha* but found the play a little too verbose and didactic. 'I contacted the playwright, asking him (whether) he (would) be available during the staging of the play and willing to work on it. To my delight he immediately agreed. I think it was the first occasion in Indian theatre when the playwright was totally involved in the process of production. Together we edited the play heavily and two (completely) new scenes were added. Doodhnath at that time regretted having published the play earlier and said that he would publish the new version, which somehow has not happened yet.'

The playwright is inspired by Bertolt Brecht and Marxism. He went underground during the Emergency. Bhanu was actively involved in the student agitation and is a sympathiser of struggling peasants and workers. He has faced the draconian Emergency laws as a theatre director.

The play provides a huge canvas to a director while conceiving his production plan. There are two parallel worlds. The world of Lord Indra – the exploiter – and the worlds of the outcasts and the deprived—the simple folk condemned to live in ignorance and darkness. Both the worlds are in conflict with each other and this provides the philosophical fulcrum to the script as well as creates tense dramatic conflict. The influence of Greek tragedy and Brechtian theatre makes the conceptualisation cumbersome. Bhanu writes in his director's note: 'The play breaks new ground at the level of style and language. Ritualistic use of poetry has created a language which is new to Hindi playwriting and theatre. Synthesis of Sanskrit dramaturgy, epic style and folk theatre has created a style which is unique.'

He tries to bring it closer to our own ritualistic tradition. Scenes of *yajna*, Vedic rituals and chanting were used as a dramatic idiom for the first time on the Hindi stage. Erotic elements and the intensity of passionate love between the lovers are portrayed through poetry. Bhanu has invented love scenes in a highly artistic way. A thick blue mattress was kept on the ground and a twenty feet-high net was spread out to create an illusion of a mountain top where lovers are engaged in a deeply romantic mood.

In *Aks-Tamasha* too, there are two levels and two worlds which are complimentary to each other. The comical is treated in folk style and the tragic world of the prince is remarkable for the synthesis of ritualistic performance and the Western theatrical tradition. In *Yum Gatha* the world of the oppressed is marked by an intense motivation. In the words of theatre critic Arvind Kumar, 'It is perhaps Bhanu's close interaction with Bheel tribes which enabled him to achieve notable success in imparting vitality to the internal revolutionary consciousness of the oppressed.' (*Nav Bharat Times, 19 November 1990*). Bhanu thoroughly knows the life of Bheels, their rituals, festivals, theatres and, above all, their intense love for liberty. Because of his intimate knowledge of these tribals Bhanu brings the world of Pururva and his people vibrantly alive. In contrast, the world of Indra is full of rich colours marked by exaggerated theatricality. The conflict between the two worlds is marked by philosophical complexity and antagonism which is irreconcilable.

Bhanu has worked hard on this project in creative collaboration with the playwright, set designer and the choreographer. He was able to bring out the very best of his talented caste with Jitender Shastri (Pururva), Himani Shivpuri (Urvashi), Ravindra Khanwilkar (Vasistha), Shrivallabh Vyas (Indra), Lokendra Trivedi (Vibhavak), Suresh Sethi (Vishavasu) and Ram Gopal Bajaj (Sanatkumar).

The portrayal of Urvashi is marked by imagination and innovation. She is a woman whose beauty is exploited by Indra for his political gains and unethical ways. In this portrayal the playwright and the director share a similar vision which projects Urvashi as the most powerful and this image lingers on in the mind of the audience. Himani, now a popular TV and film actress, has created many memorable portraits while she was the NSD Repertory artist in plays *Mitro Marjani* and *Desdemona*.

On his choice of the open-air theatre instead of the proscenium, Bhanu explains, 'The canvas of the play is big and multi-dimensional, which will not fit into any proscenium stage. In fact, I'm more comfortable (with) open-air spaces rather than closed auditoriums. I am most uncomfortable working on the proscenium. But in the Indian situation you are mostly unfortunately dumped in the proscenium theatre. But whenever I have an opportunity I would work in open-air and mostly in an environmental setting and space [*sic*]. Informal spaces attract me most.'

In the words of Dr Kamlesh Datt Tripthi, a scholar, 'Here is a new play, with its full controversiality, demanding a new theatre.' Bhanu created this new theatre with a new theatre language and a new perspective of contemporary Indian theatre, which was deeply rooted in our soil and the consciousness of our people with subtle nuances of a larger, universal appeal.

Ek Sapne Ki Maut: recreation of an American classic

"We want to give ourselves, and yet all we train for is to take, as though nothing less will keep the world at a safe distance. Every day we contradict our will to create, which is to give. The end of man is not security, but without security we are without the elementary condition of humaneness.

"The reason Death of a Salesman, *for instance, left such a strong impression was that it set forth unremittingly the picture of a man who was not even especially "good" but those situations made clear that at the bottom we are alone, valueless, without even the elements of a human …*

—Arthur Miller

In the *Death of a Salesman* Bhanu Bharti invests Indian ethos and Indian economic and social prospective without destroying the atmospheric colour and the essence of this great American play by Arthur Miller. Its premier was held at Shri Ram Centre, New Delhi, on 6 December 1982. Written in 1948 against the socio-economic forces at work with capitalism stifling the voices of individual freedom, robbing the masses of their dignity and human essence, this play is immensely popular in India. Bhanu liberated his production of *Death of a Salesman* through his collaboration with J.N. Kaushal who adapted it from the original, emphasising the elements inherent in this masterpiece of the twentieth century which have been staged in most countries of the world, including its historical staging in Beijing under the direction of the playwright himself. It keeps on moving the audience all over the world the way it moved the audience when they saw it for the first time in 1949. *Ek Sapne Ki Maut* is considered Bhanu's rare creative effort to transform a foreign work into Indian context.

In a long conversion with him, he highlights the following points that he kept in mind while giving an Indian dimension to *Death of a Salesman* in which Willy Loman, the protagonist, becomes Ramdas, Linda the wife of Willy, becomes Savitri and their sons – Biff and Happy – are presented as Bannu and Harshi.

'Though in the 1980s we were following the concept of mixed economy but one could well see the economic forces of capitalism gaining ground and pressure on the polity to open the market for a free economy. It was post-Emergency period and the influence of America had begun to tell on the country. We had had the experience of Sanjay Gandhi and a right-wing politician, Morarjibhai Desai, emerging as a choice for the prime minister in place of Jagjivan Ram. This was also the time for a huge migration to foreign countries, particularly to America and Western Europe … in pursuit of materialistic gains. The experiment of a socialistic pattern of society and the dream of Sampurn Kranti – the Total Revolution – propounded by Jaiprakash Narain totally failed. It was in this scenario I chose to do a play like *Death of a Salesman* in Indian adaptation. You can well call it a forewarning of things in the offing ...'

The dramatic action involves people who have settled in Delhi after the Partition. The protagonist belongs to a trading Punjabi community which has settled in Old Rajinder Nagar. At that time refugee colonies at Rajinder Nagar, Patel Nagar in west Delhi and South Extension, Greater Kailash in south Delhi were emerging as priced colonies. Hard work was considered as a key to success and one could achieve respect in the family and society when one was successful as a businessman and failure in business resulted in fall of reputation. The *nouveau riche* emerging class of refugees uprooted from its socio-economic and cultural mores, embraced a new culture marked by personal aggrandizement, mad pursuit for materialism and narcissist traits. They have little patience for the respect of human values. In the words of J.N. Kaushal, 'We are entering the same phase of development now which Miller had observed forty years ago. With our *nouveau riche* and their new-found wealth, we have the same ... problems today.'

While capturing sounds and tracing the daily routine of a refugee family caught in the web of self-preservation, their food habits and filial conflicts and the continued fall into the pit of misery, Bhanu added that the inhabitants of these colonies were obsessed with bubble dream; it was the kind of dream the Americans had dreamt in the '30s and '40s. Willy Loman's brother Ben goes to Alaska and the brother of Ramdas, Balwant, go to Africa. Both strike gold.

The basic structure of the original is kept intact. The dramatic action involves the twenty-four hours in the life of Ramdas which leads to his suicide. As in the original, the action moves in two time levels—the past and present. This hard-working salesman has a modest success. Once upon a time his son adored him as a model father. Now in his early sixties, he is fired by the firm he served for more than three decades. He is actually feeling a sense of guilt and failure in life. Now he in not able to pay the instalments of insurance and his house is still mortgaged. The past and the present mingle. On the surface, the play appears to be simple. To differentiate the two time levels, a kind of expressionistic environment is evoked. 'The simplicity of the play, however, quickly dissolves into filial ambiguity, civic paradox and the philosophical complexities'. (*The Cambridge Companion to Arthur Miller*, pp 60)

Discussing the original staging by Elia Kazan with setting and lighting designed by Jo Mielziner, Bhanu said that the playwright broke out from the steelframe of Russian master Stanislavsky. Through his multi-level sets, music and lighting and the state of mind of the protagonist, who is not only losing his dreams and goals but is also not able to accept his defeat in a dog-eats-dog world, Bhanu reveals honestly its socio-economic overtones. 'The stage of Shri Ram Centre is not huge; it was a challenge. The milieu I was dealing with was very fresh. When I decided to do the adaptation of this play everyone thought that I had gone nuts. *Death of the Salesman* was conceived as a typically American experience alien to all other cultures and societies. Even the people who were moved by the human tragedy of Miller thought that it only happens in America, and fail to see any universal connection. Therefore I think this is my success in bringing it to our own experiences, making it an authentic and dramatically artistic statement of our time.

'I got hold of J.N. Kaushal to do this adaptation because I thought being a Punjabi himself he would be able to render it effectively. I wanted the refugee mentality and ethos to be projected. I worked very closely with him and suggested how various situations are to be adapted and wanted the woman of the house to use Punjabi and not Hindi. Kaushal was baffled as everybody else when I asked him not to translate but to adapt the play in the milieu I thought would give the authenticity needed.

'I wanted the woman to speak in Punjabi—the kind of Punjabi being spoken in the families of migrant Punjabies and the day-to-day conversation. At places there are English words used by male characters who speak in Hindi.'

In Bhanu's production, Savitri (Linda) plays the central role. For him she is not a marginalised character as some critics treat her. 'I saw her in my production as a strong character who is the conscience keeper of the family. She gives some meaning to the family which is fast disintegrating with the head of the family gradually moving towards the end of his life. I ended the play with this woman shrieking 'Babuji' as the salesman commits suicide. The curtain comes down while her shrieks of 'Babuji' keep on vibrating the auditorium. Pratima Kazmi as Savitri came as a strong actress in the production. It was she who brought out the human tragedy in a most poignant manner. Lalit Behl as Ramdas gives an outstanding performance.'

Bhanu's production is also remarkable for its undercurrents that reveal the evils of capitalistic mode of production which "brutalises the unsuccessful" and dehumanises man. With the market forces operating in an unfettered manner and the *nouveau riche* culture replacing moral and social commitments, the relevance of *Ek Sapne Ki Maut* has acquired tremendous appeal.

The production reflects Bhanu's quest for new techniques of dramatic expression drawn from modern theatrical practice, reflecting his broad artistic range.

He worked hard with his cast to make them understand the philosophical and social implication of Miller's *Death of a Salesman*, resulting in their inspired performances. As a result of their brilliant portrayals some of the cast members – Pratima Kazmi and Lalit Behl – were selected by NSD's Repertory Company as performers. For them it was a real hounour to have been selected by the Repertory despite being non-NSD graduates.

Katha Kahi Ek Jale Ped Ne: Bhanu the playwright

A play is a slice of life artistically put on the boards.

—Jean Jullen

Experimentalism in the arts always reflects historical conditions, always indicates profound dissatisfaction with established modes, always is a groping toward a new age.

—Eric Bentley

Bhanu Bharti's quest for a new perspective for contemporary Indian theatre not only reflects in his consistent exploration of an ingenious idiom but in his plays too, which do not follow the beaten track of conventional playwriting in Hindi. His plays have a new format and new content—freshness and a dramatic sweep. Not satisfied with the current crop of Hindi plays, he mostly wrote his own plays as both originals and adaptations. It is heartening to know that scholars of Hindi dramaturgy have started to study his works seriously. A research scholar based in Puducherry has been writing a research thesis on his plays. Some of his plays have also been adapted in a few regional Indian languages. The broad features of his works are: a fable-like narrative flow, its contemporary appeal with many layers that makes his plays a work of complex art.

While in Japan as a scholar to study Japanese traditional theatre, Bhanu did not limit his study to the traditional, classical and modern

Japanese theatre. A voracious reader, he studied Japanese literature, especially post-World War II literary works. He read across an avant garde magazine in which he came across a short story by Kijima Hajime entitled *A Story Told by a Scorched Tree*. 'The original story is short,' Bhanu goes on to say. 'It fascinated me because of its multi-faceted meanings and layers. On the surface it is very simple, natural and it unfolds itself in an unaffected manner. I decided to write a full-length play as soon as I returned to India,' says Bhanu.

The interesting thing about this play is that its characters are monkeys and dogs. On a superficial view it resembles George Orwell's *Animal Farm*. An allegory of the Soviet system, it is a satire on communism and tends to be propagandist in tone which limits its appeal. Bhanu's play *Katha Kahi Ek Jale Ped Ne* has wider appeal. Its dramatis personae are monkeys; yet they are not monkeys in a literal sense and nor do they reflect the process of evolution of man from the animal kingdom. They have consciousness and aspirations. This is a world dominated by a monkey queen who is fired with the malignant desire to attain immortality and youth. The satire on totalitarianism is subtle. Beneath the apparent fable there lies many layers, investing the animal characters with meanings which have contemporary relevance. It mirrors the eternal conflict between forces of creation and distruction. It is also an indictment of dictatorship and the folly of dictators to perpetuate their authority through brute force. In the words of Sarveshwar Dayal Saxena, a critic and playwright, '*Katha Kahi Ek Jale Ped Ne*, is, in fact, the story of the destiny of man. If man expands consciousness in society and creation he creates a new man, if he does not rise above him, destruction of man and humanity is certain. Only a scorched tree will survive to tell the story of man.' (*Dinman*, 5-11 July 1981).

Bhanu has retained the apparent simplicity and engaging thematic elements of the original story. Jale Ped (The scorched tree) is cast in the role of a narrator which comments between the scenes, enriching the narrative philosophically and re-enforcing the curiosity of the audience. The main characters are the queen, Kanchuki; a minister, Sukheetori-me; a painter and the protagonist and Sonotori-me, a painter and confidant of Kanchuki. There are two mutually hostile groups consisting of fourteen monkeys and six dogs.

The scorched tree tells the story of a distant past when monkeys were more powerful than dogs. It was the monkey queen who ruled the jungles. She was intelligent and was endowed with unparalleled beauty. Apprehensive of the possibility that her offspring may not be as beautiful as she was she decided not to conceive any child.

With no authority to challenge her rule, she is preoccupied with the idea of projecting her beauty to the masses in order to keep them under the sway of her authority and be treated as the ultimate symbol of monkey civilisation and the source of ultimate power. She decides to project the idea through her paintings. A painting competition is held to paint the queen. As a ruler with a keen eye to appreciate a work of art, it is not an easy task to please her. One by one most of the paintings are rejected and the painters humiliated. However, the queen approves one painting by Sukeetori-me and subsequently he is declared court painter. The queen's portraits are displayed in the kingdom. In due course, the painter becomes disgusted with the situation and his paintings fall short of the queen's expectations. One day she expresses her displeasure by throwing away a painting by the court painter. 'What is it that you have painted? What is wrong with you?' asks the queen angrily.

Dissatisfied with himself and unable to express his inner anguish, Sukheetori tells the queen that he wants her permission to go on a journey to an unknown place as he is sad and tired. The queen allows him to proceed and asks him to return soon. It is rumoured that the queen has exiled him because as a royal painter he failed miserably to deliver.

A cunning Kanchuki employs Sonotori-me in his place, with an ulterior motive. The queen is not satisfied with the paintings by the new royal painter and longs for the return of Sukheetori-me.

Scene seven opens with a narration by the scorched tree.

Sonotori strives hard to impress the queen but far from being satisfied the queen grows increasingly impatient and irritated to see his paintings and eagerly awaits Sukheetori-me's return. Meanwhile Sukheetori-me has been travelling through many distant lands. He travels from one monkey kingdom to another, including the regions inhabited by baboons and giraffes. In these places he hears stories about a creature who is a monkey and yet not fully one. He comes to know that this strange creature is called 'man'. In the course of his journey he has learnt several languages, including that of the fish and the birds. Finally a day came when Sukheetori-me decides to return to the kingdom of the monkey queen.

In his absence Sonotori-me with the connivance of Kanchuki has been functioning as the royal painter but the monkey queen longs to be painted by Sukheetori-me.

The day comes when the original court painter arrives. There are efforts by Sonotori-me and Kanchuki to distract the queen and falsely implicate Sukheetori-me of poisoning the fish in the lakes but the queen is delighted to see Sukheetori-me after many years and rejects all false complaints against him.

Addressing the assembled crowd, the queen declares Sukheetori-me to be a symbol of national glory and honour. Sukheetori-me's arrival follows a series of meetings between him and the queen who is eager to know about his travels and be painted by him. She wants to know about the creature which is a monkey and yet not fully one—a clever and secure mortal with a longer life span than other living creatures. To the dismay of the queen he tells her that he has not come across any living being to be immortal. The queen's earlier jubiliation on meeting him after many years gradually gives way to disenchantment. The painter finds himself agonisingly unable to paint the queen and capture her exquisitely beautiful face. In a lonely reflective moment with a heart full of conflicting ideas, he says to himself: 'Your paintings of a pure heart he gives mocking a smile'.

The painter becomes increasingly aware of the smallness, worthlessness and ugliness of the monkey queen. Whenever he forces himself to portray the queen, he only perceives her inner ugliness and brutality. The queen wishes that she should be portrayed as the paragon of beauty.

Finally, Sukheetori-me starts painting her and the final image on the canvas turns out to be a dreadful one. An enraged queen orders the painter to be thrown into the dungeons.

Gradually the queen grows old, weak and is on the verge of death. Fierce battles ensue between the monkeys and the dogs and the forest is set on fire. The play ends with the scorched tree beseeching people to remember the paintings by the court painter even if they do not remember his name, as those paintings manifested the eternal struggle between the forces of life and death.

A multi-layered work of art, it is an interesting tale of the monkey queen's futile desire to become immortal on the surface. At another level, it is a comment on dictatorship. There are three types of characters––monkeys, dogs and a scorched tree. There is an underlying layer of dramatic conflict.

In the words of Jaydev Taneja, Hindi drama historian and critique: '*Katha Kahi Ek Jale Ped Ne* projects the story of evolution from antiquity to the primitive ape civilisation and modern human society in a vivid way that we at once identify the contradictions and issues of our own life and milieu.'

The play is a post-Emergency production. Some critics described the play as an allusion to Indira Gandhi and her Emergency regime. Interestingly, a few painters, including M.F. Husain painted Indira Gandhi as the goddess Durga, the destroyer of all evil. Husain's paintings were displayed at Triveni Art Gallery during the Emergency. The National Gallery of Modern Art received verbal orders from one of the Emergency power centres to purchase those particular Husain paintings. But the then director refused to obey.

In any case, *Katha Kahi Ek Jale Ped Ne* has a universal appeal. Its relevance will be felt whenever dictatorial regime anywhere in the world deprives people of their rights of freedom of expression and creativity. A highly innovative dramatic piece, it reflects man's ethical and political concerns. Indeed, Bhanu has enriched the contemporary Hindi dramaturgy by writing a multi-layered work of dramatic art.

Chandrama Singh Urf Chamku: humiliation, resistance and conspiracy

The chief characters in these stories – the mad man, Kung i-chi, Jun-tu, Ah Q and the rest – are all unfortunates in an abnormal society. Lusun made a strong protest against their unhappy fate, and mercilessly exposed and attacked the forces that oppressed them, at the same time giving true expression to their wishes, demands and potential strengths. He showed that the only way out was through changing society – through revolution.

—Feng Hsueh-Feng

The thrust for freedom is the quality in tragedy which exalts. The revolutionary questioning of the stable environment is what terrifies. In no way is the common man debarred from such thoughts or such actions.

—Arthur Miller

In *Katha Kahi Ek Jale Ped Ne* Bhanu Bharti uses monkeys and dogs in an allegorical style to depict the eternal conflict between the progressive and regressive forces. In *Chandrama Singh Urf Chamku* he dramaties the suffering of the landless against the backdrop of the Naxalbari movement, forcefully advocating man's need for freedom from oppression for the creation of new life in a new society, replacing the old and rotten one. Inspired by Lu Hsun's immortal work *The True Story Of Ah Q*, *Chandrama Singh Urf Chamku* depicts Indian situations, dramatis personae and plot which are identifiable, evoking a sense of immediacy inevents.

According to Lu Hsun, one of the greatest writers of the world and the father of new Chinese literature, *The True Story of Ah Q* is told against the failed Chinese revolution of 1911, illustrating its utter failure to mobile peasants, criticising its leadership formed by bourgeoisie while depicting the tragic life of the dispossessed as in *Ah Q*. Analysing the failure of the Naxalbari movement, Bhanu explains that the main cause of its failure was that it was imposed from above by well-meaning, highly-sensitive and intelligent young people from the elite class. They had a romantic idea of armed revolution. They wanted to liberate peasantry from the bondage of feudalism, which continues to perpetuate its oppression, despite sixty years of Independence. The land reforms acts remained mostly on paper. The political leadership did not bother to educate farmers, particularly the landless ones, to make them politically conscious. The objective conditions were rife but the adventurism of leadership resulted in violence and oppression let loose by the state. Bhanu further states that today the movement is in a fragmented state, localised in areas like Chhattisgarh and Andhra Pradesh. He observes that the feudal ruling class continues to exploit peasants. The tribal culture and economy are being ruined by vested interests with a view to divide the people; the mainstream parties are busy with their vote banks based on caste, region and religion. In such a rural landscape, the characters in *Chandrama Singh* are alive which impart authenticity and vibrancy to the script.

Our protagonist Chandrama echoes the voice of the rural poor, demanding justice and freedom from oppression. As a common man, he dares to question the inhuman system in his own way attaining a tragic death.

The play is set in a village situated on the belt of the Son river in Bihar. In fact this was one of the villages where the Naxalbari movement created an upheaval in 1968. The rich landlords, some of them owning 2000 acres of land were known for their blatant exploitation of the landless, subjecting them to spine-breaking labour. When Naxalites declared some of these villages as 'liberated' the landless and poor peasants grabbed the land of feudal lords. These areas were under the control of Naxalites for some time. The landlords fled their villages, terrified by the call of the Naxalites to the farmers to annihilate 'class enemies' which resulted in the murder of several landlords. This invited repression by the state which restored the confiscated land to the land owners and the short-lived movement was ruthlessly crushed.

Little is known about Chandrama's parentage. He is one of the poorest of the village poor. He is exploited as a labourer, insulated and humiliated while the villagers make him a butt of ridicule. But he is not a village fool. Whenever he is teased and often beaten for fun and shooed away, he feels deeply hurt and too weak to retaliate. To escape the cruelty of the villagers, he buys and drinks cheap alcohol, mostly on credit. Even here he is ridiculed. Chandrama retaliates and boasts, 'At the house of Babusahib, preparations are being made to celebrate the arrival of their son from the city who has passed his fourteenth class. The mistress of the house has cooked rich food and asked me to visit them frequently ...'

(Translated extract in sequence from the play):

Tilanga-One: 'Yes. Yes, she would definitely offer you rich food. After all, you are their son-in-law!' (*sarcastically*).

Chandrama: 'Why not! After all I belong to their caste. There was a time when we were stronger and richer as compared to them. Now, our stars are bad.'

Tilanga-One: (*Addressing Thakedar, the owner of the liquor shop*) 'Are you listening? Chamku claims that he is a relative of Babusahib and had once been richer than him.'

(Everyone laughs at Chandrama)

Thakedar: 'Why not! This is why he is always welcome at the house of Babusahib!'

Chandrama: 'Look here, Thakedar. I am Chandrama Singh. Call me by this name.'

Thakedar: 'Yes, yes, Thakur Chandrama Singh! You are related to the family of ...'

Babusahib: 'Isn't it right?'
(Everybody laughs)
Tilanga-One: 'Very good—Thakur Chandrama Singh!'

This is how Chamku tries to deceive himself. Soon, the news of the liquor shop reaches Thakur Dinanath Singh, whom villagers call 'Babusahib'. Chandrama is summoned by Babusahib who is sitting on a bench. His graduate son is sitting in a chair. Muscleman Radho Singh is also present. Village police chowkidar and Chandrama Singh sit on the ground. Thakur Sahib is visibly angry.

Thakur Saheb: How dare you say that you are related to us?

The son of Thakur: You worthless fellow.

Babu Sahib: What does he say? Thakur Chandrma Singh!

(A furious Thakur slaps him twice)

Shame to your Thakurhood! You mother fucker. (*Chandrama does not resist; he allows himself to be beaten.*)

The son of Thakur: Leave him Babuji. Why are you fighting with him?

Babusahib: Utter once again that and you are not our relative. You will be lynched.

Madho Singh: Go away from here. If you try to utter any nonsense you will not be spared. (*He kicks him*). Run ...

There are several scenes like this in which Chandrama is beaten and abused. On these occasions he has a strong desire to retaliate. He is torn between his desire to revolt and to quietly submit to his tormentors. On his part, he also tries to ridicule and fight against those who happen to be weaker than himself. He pinches the cheeks of a poor nun and unabashedly asks a female servant of the Thakurs – a widow – to sleep with him. He picks up a quarrel with Budhwa, a landless labourer like him and beats Kalu Muchchad whom he laughs at, when the latter runs out of fear.

Considering it his moral victory, Chandrama deceives himself. When the female servant reports the matter to the Thakur, Chandrama is beaten mercilessly – the widow making a hue and cry all this while – alleging that he has ruined her moral reputation.

Occasionally he is beaten by the police and village hooligans. Often on such occasions, he indulges in day dreams. In an aside he once says, while furious with the son of Thakur, '…having passed the 14th class he thinks of himself as the Collector. If I am to beget a son he would become a more senior officer than you are….'

Once he wins a lot of money through gambling at a fair. A stampede takes place and a policeman gets hold of Chandrama, beats him and in the process he loses all his gambling smoney in the chaos. Thrashed and deprived of his money, Chandrama is bitter and resentful. He says to himself, 'They not only beat me but also took my money. It is all because of the bad times. I had so much money … an amount I had never seen before. My luck is bad. I am a worm, a worm in a drain.'

He is a frequent visitor to the liquor shop and finds some escape from the brutality of the people he works for and earns a pittance in exchange. He is also insulted at the shop by the owner of the liquor shop and some village ruffians for his inability to pay for the liquor.

Disgusted with village life he goes to the city and works as a domestic help in the house of a senior bureaucrat. Later, he joins a petty thief and returns to his village with a booty in order to escape from the police. For the first time in his life, he receives a warm welcome. The villagers consider him to be a rich man. Chandrama distributes his valuable clothes to the villagers, spends money on liquor, and in a few days he becomes his old self, inviting ridicule from one and all.

Meanwhile, there are echoes of Naxal slogans and a strong wave of revolt against the feudal ruling class. Chandrama who is insulted and beaten for no fault of his is keen to know about the Naxalite movement. It gives him an inner strength to revolt, which is reflected in the following dialogue between Chandrama and the liquor shop owner. Even after repeated requests by Chandrama to give him a small quantity of liquor on credit, the owner refuses.

Chandrama: *Arrey*, give a little bit.

Thekedar: Go away from here or else … (*he moves towards him holding a piece of log. Chandrama runs. The customers sitting in the shop laugh at his plight. He sees the lean and thin Budhwa approaching them. He turns angry, raises his hand and suddenly starts shouting*: *Inqilab zindabad*!!

A startled Budhwa leaves silently.

Chandrama had an intense hatred for landlords and an inner urge to revolt, which inspire him to project the image of Naxalbari as larger than life. The rumour about the arrival of the Red Army in the village is a ray of hope for him. The oppressed are happy and the landed gentry is terrified. Somehow, villagers are under the impression that Chandrama is associated with the Naxalbari movement and he is treated with fear and respect. Police chowkidar Pujan addresses Chandrama in a respectful tone and invites him to have tea with him.

Chandrama has no home and is forced to take refuge in the corner of a temple, bearing with the insults of the priest. Now that Chandrama is treated as a Naxalite, the priest goes out of his way to pamper him. Chandrama assures him that he should not fear about revolt. He says, 'Revolutionaries are deeply religious. They worship Naxalbari. Yes, of course, they are against double dealers like you.' The priest offers him sweets to win him over.

The feudal ruling class devises ways to meet the Naxalbari challenge. The acts of conspiracy are devised secretly. If Chandrama is a self-styled Naxalite, the educated son of Babusahib and a section of the landlords too, masquerade as Naxalite leaders. Chandrama comes to know about the landlords in the guise of Naxalites; confused he tries to join them. But he is thrown out of the room in which the so called Naxalites are having their meeting.

An insulted and enraged Chandrama is finally branded as a hardcore Naxatlite while he is in the temple—surrounded by the police as well as the villagers and the feudal ruling class. After repeated warnings by police officers, he emerges from the temple with his arms raised.

Nonetheless, several guns fire at him and his body crumples to the ground. On the orders of the officer, a policeman puts a country made pistol in his hand—to proclaim the incident as the death of a dreaded Naxatlite in an encounter.

Bhanu uses the cinematic style to compose scenes. He lays stress on dramatic action and uses less dialogue. Structurally, the script reads tight and has a swift pace. There is a juxtaposition of various scenes to create a montage. In an open space at times action takes place in different locales simultaneously. This device imparts to the play a remarkable expressive power, liberating it from the tyranny of verbosity. The play is a departure from the Ibsenite concept which is basically dialogue-centric. 'The plays by Mohan Rakesh and Vijay Tendulkar are dialogue oriented. I tried to use minimum dialogue. My emphasis was on visuals', said Bhanu. In Lu Hsun's original story, he creates humour in bleak situations. Bhanu's script captures the comic elements of the original. As far as the treatment of time and space are concerned, Bhanu's approach is innovative. The action flows rhythmically with the play, tuned to the pulse of village life with its antagonistic contradictions. In the open space the whole village is conceived, which enables the action to flow seamlessly.

In *Chandrama Singh Urf Chamku*, Bhanu has structurally, thematically and aesthetically helped evolve a new dramatic genre—little known in Hindi playwriting.

Naachni: feudal theatre of decadence

In a decaying society, art, if it is truthful, must also reflect decay. And unless it wants to break faith with its social function, art must show the world as changeable. And help to change it.

—Ernst Fischer

Experiment in the arts always reflects historical conditions, always indicates profound dissatisfaction with established modes, always is a groping toward a new age.

—Eric Bentley

With his life devoted to the arts and having witnessed many classical dance recitals by the country's leading dance exponents Bhanu Bharti is much fascinated by the dance of Sitara Devi. He has also been reading about the lives and art of foreign ballet dancers like Isadora Duncan, the mother of modern and contemporary dance. He planned to present the dancers' world on the stage, dramatising not only their arts but also their lives. 'This idea was in my subconscious,' says Bhanu. One day I received a small book written by a research scholar on Naachni, a traditional dance form practised (along) the Bihar and West Bengal border. The writer had selected some dancers of this form and written their life stories. This was a sketchy work but heart-rending. I was moved to read the pathetic story of these dancers. Through the book

I came to know that Naachni (dancers) mostly come from poor homes, often kidnapped by a dance *ustad* called Rasik who trains these girls as dancers. After training they perform at village fairs, (but) their earnings are grabbed by the Rasik. Sexually exploited, the more voluptuous ones and skilled dancers are invited by landlords.

'Though they are in great demand as entertainers, they are shunned by society. When they die, their legs are fastened with a rope … (and) the body is dragged and thrown far away from the village, left there to be eaten by dogs and wolves. This revelation was a shock to me. I decided to write a play (about) the savagery of a decaying society. But it was not easy; the character of a Naachni is essentially that of a dancer, capable of mesmerising crowds at a fair.... The performer to be cast in this role should be a highly trained and experienced dancer. She should also be a fine stage actress to project the multi-layered emotional world of (a) Naachni. Fortunately in Sindhu Mishra we have a talented dancer-actress. So I decided to write a one-actress play', Bhanu explains.

Bhanu suggests an austere stage design for the presentation of the play, with a black curtain serving as a backdrop. A stage approximately four feet wide runs from one end of the backdrop to another. Two chairs and a stool are placed on this stage and there is no interval in the play. When the play draws to its end, the black curtain is removed and is replaced by a mirror-like backdrop on which Naachni's multiple reflections appear—symbolising her indomitable will power to survive in a cruel world and making her private world public. This is how Naachni and her dance become eternal.

The play begins with Naachni in conversation with her daughter who does not exist. All alone in a highly reflective state of mind, Naachni sees the daughter in her mind's eye. Gradually she pours out the details of her troubled life, the men that came in her life and her dance that has kept her alive through thick and thin. She also tells her daughter who her father was—a drunkard and a parasite who forced Naachni to leave home and her baby girl and go out to dance and earn money. She tells her daughter that while she was absent from home the father sold the baby to earn money for his liquor. When she attacked him with the fury of a tigress, questioning him about the missing child, he falsely reported that the girl had died and produced the villagers as witness to the baby's death. Her narrative is punctuated with dances which are vigorous, elegant and captivating.

The Naachni tells her invisible daughter about the faint memories of her childhood. Growing up in a far-away mountain village, she loved nature and dancing as a young girl. She remembers being in tune with the grandeur of the forest all around—bright and colourful with an abundance of green trees, flowers and butterflies. 'I also used to dance as a free bird. One day an ugly man with big moustaches took me away, destroying my innocence and the happy world.'

This man taught her how to dance in public and took her to fairs where she would perform. He would beat her and starve her whenever she defied him. She goes on to relate how once, while she was performing, a handsome man came riding on a horse, caught hold of her, lifted her up and galloped away. Nobody dared to stop him. She was happy to be free from the clutches of the ugly man.

This handsome man was a Rasik who trained girls to dance, introducing them to the profession of Naachni. He was a lover, experienced dance teacher and physically strong. Undergoing rigorous training, she took up the Naachni profession and was known as Kisookibai. Soon she became much sought-after at popular fairs and in demand with the wealthy zamindars and the Thakurs. 'I was fortunate enough to get him,' she speaks of the new Rasik in her life to her daughter. 'He was my lover, full of passion. His art was as great as his physical strength. He was truly kanhaiya, a lover.'

Kisookibai's popularity as a dancer reached far and wide. She was flooded with invitations to dance. One day she was very happy and disclosed to the Rasik that she was pregnant, hoping that her lover would reciprocate her feelings and would be happy too.

(Extract from the play in English translation)

Rasik: Are you in your right mind? Is this the time to get involved in this muddle? Right now you have to dance; you have to maintain your body. If it loses its suppleness, nobody would be interested in you.

Naachni: What are you saying, Rasik? What for do I need this body if not allowed to become a mother?

Rasik: There is enough time for that. Don't forget that you are a Naachni; not a home maker to give birth to a child.

Naachni was forced to drink a bitter concoction. After abortion, she became seriously ill. It took her long to recover and dance. Once again she found herself close to Rasik who under her influence stopped indulging in criminal activities but was soon murdered by his rivals. Kisookibai lost her senses, danced in frenzy and the people watching her for a Devi and started worshiping her.

Overcoming her grief and loneliness, she resumes her dance. In her conversation with her imaginary daughter, she says, '... for me dance used to be everything—joy, sorrow, weeping and singing. It is only dance that kept me alive. If I had not been dancing, I would have died long ago. It is not difficult to die. What was hard was to remain alive, to dance and to be able to dance.'

The last man in the life of Naachni is Kapoor Sahib who owned an itinerant dance company. He respects artists and their arts but a change in public taste and the onslaught of cinema-related entertainment results in the bankruptcy of his company. Insulted and disowned by his family Kapoor Sahib spends his last days with Naachni.

At one level, the play is a severe indictment of a male dominated society which treats women like commodity. While addressing her daughter, Naachni says '... look at us! We are deprived of what is available to men. That is why women have always been weak. What justice had Ramachandra meted out to Sita? When she came out unhurt by fire, she was left in a forest!' Naachni found women in contemporary times more vulenarable than during the time of the *Mahabharata*. 'Krishna was there to protect Draupadi. Today there is no Krishna. Men have made the poor Naachni an object of entertainment and sexual exploitation but at the same time untouchable. In case of her death, nobody touches her body because she is impure and a source of evil, a sinner who does not deserve burial or cremation as per rituals. Her body is to be clawed and devoured by jackals and vultures. The image often haunts her in her nightmares and she wishes to avoid death by dancing eternally.

The play unfolds in a historical perspective. It presents social classes and the changing political landscape. The action takes place at a time when the country's struggle for freedom gains strength with each passing day. With the departure of British imperialism the old ruling class of landlords and the rulers of the Indian princely states became relics of the past.

❧

With the changing times, people's perception of entertainment also changed. Film songs and dances became more popular, which led to the gradual fading out of traditional singers and dancers. These changes and socially conditioned worldviews are implicitly expressed in the play. It also indicates the decadence of feudalism. Though the feudal ruling class is presented as a patron of art and culture, the fact that they indulge in concubinage and enslave women is shown in poor light. The bankruptcy and death of Kapoor Sahib suggest the social need for new art forms as the old forms gradually die a natural death with the passing out of the old social order.

As a solo performer Sindhu Mishra as Naachni held the audience spellbound for one and a half hours. She lent depth and subtlety to her portrayal, embellishing her acting with dance which was elegant, vigorous and seemingly effortless.

In the climactic scene she dances ecstatically and intensely, as if driven by a deep inner creative urge, creating an image that defies her rotten condition, overcomes her fear of death and transforms her image into a celebration of life and creativity.

Interactions with actors

Stanislavsky insisted that art cannot be taught, that the most one can do is prepare a person, create the most favourable conditions for inspiration ....

... My aim was simply to stress that the solution is a chain of logically justified and warranted actions, that in the chain of events the inner life always has its outward expression and there is always a complex relationship between words and physical actions, and pauses and details can express the most involved emotional experiences.

—Georgi Tovstonogov

Contemporary theatre has three pillars—playwright, director and actor. A harmonious relationship between these three pillars is essential for the success of a theatrical production. There was a time when director was not considered necessary. Written dialogues were the main expressive means and these were conveyed by live actors on the stage. There was a coordinator and a manager to present the play. Often this job was performed by the playwright himself. Theatre was mostly known after playwrights as in Shakespeare's theatre, Moliere's theatre and Gorky's theatre. But with the introduction of technology and great theatrical innovations made by creative persons like Edward Gordon Craig (1872-1966) – English director, designer and theorist, and Adolph Appia (1862-1928) – Swiss stage designer and theorist, the nature of theatre changed. Theatre was coming to life with its creative horizon widening and acting style was undergoing revolutionary changes. Directors, actors and teachers like Konstantin Sergeyevich Stanislavsky (1865-1938), Bertolt Brecht (1898-1956) and Vsevolovlod Meyerhold (1874-1940), evolved new theories to enrich and make creative theatrical art more complex, calling for highly educated and imaginative theatre artiststs. This creative person with his knowledge and practical experience in all aspects of the theatre came to be known as the director who has acquired vital force in harmonising all aspects of theatrical art and in interpreting the written text to reflect his own times. Theatre came to be known after the name of the stage director. Today it is being referred to as Peter Brook's theatre, Shombhu Mitra's theatre, Alkazi's theatre, B.N. Shah's theatre, Mohan Maharishi's theatre, Karanth's theatre and Bhanu Bharti's theatre. It is also called as Brook's Shakespeare and Bhanu's Ibsen.

The hallmark of a director is that he should be a voracious reader of literature and current affairs and should think imaginatively. He should faithfully interpret the author and find out a synthesis between his interpretations and that of the interpretation of the actor. His vital role in theatre often turns him into a despot. Edward Gordon's concept of an actor being 'little more than a glorified puppet' is not a practical view. He cannot enjoy unbridled freedom. Despite his restrictions, he remains the main force in the production. In the words of Georgi Tovstonogov, a pioneer of Soviet theatre: 'A theatre cannot be without a director, for it is the director who plots the theatre's creative part. Every single matter of stage art without exception depends on him and it is he who bears the main responsibility for a production. He is to blame if the play is bad, if the acting is not genuine, if the audience laughs in the wrong places. He speaks for the whole theatre company, and his opinion is taken more seriously as a rule than that of any actor. He is approached with all sorts of questions connected with the production and is bound to give an answer. The director has numerous duties, but also considerable rights.' Despite the supremacy of the director, he conveys his vision through actors and actors have their own visions of their roles. Is there a contradiction between these two visions? Every director has his own method of working with his performers and theatre is a collective art. Every director faces problems and every director finds his own resolution to create an artistic whole.

Bhanu Bharti is a highly creative director. In a way he is an all-round theatre artist—actor, dramatist, director and designer. He is well-read and exposed to a wide range of theatrical practices—Japanese classical and modern theatre, Bheel tribal theatre, Sanskrit classical theatre and modern realistic theatre. He has worked with amateurs, professionals and tribal artists. Here he recounts his experience working with some of the performers who have acted under his direction in some of his landmark productions:

'An actor basically acts with his instinct; thinking actors are very few. He or she is partial to himself or herself and his or her role; the actor does not think beyond the character he portrays. He or she starts consciously or unconsciously to glorify it because he or she has a central concern which can be disastrous for the production in totality. An actor has a natural instinct of exhibitionism; he or she likes to show off and very easily be carried away by the response from the audience. I have seen many good actors slipping into playing to the gallery; there are few actors that resist that temptation. I have seen in many productions when open to the public, that the director is no longer involved in the production. The actor takes over the play on a day to day basis. The actor loses focus; at times the production becomes lopsided. Therefore it becomes necessary for the director to involve himself in the production on a day-to-day basis to maintain checks and balances.

'I shall like to discuss some of the actors like Naseeruddin Shah, Surekha Sikri, Om Puri, Uttara Baokar, Jyoti Deshpande, Sindhu Mishra, Mahendra Mewati, Pratima Kazmi, Lalit Behl, Himani Shivpuri, Subrata Kumar Dutta and Shrivardhan Trivedi.

'Casting is one of the most challenging tasks a director has to face. The criteria are different with each play. Mostly there are two situations. You know the actors and their capabilities because they have worked with you or you have seen them working on the stage. In that case, it becomes far easier for you to cast them in a play because you know beforehand their working methodology, their range as an actor, their strong points and weaknesses. There is another situation when you do not know the actors working with you well enough. So you begin with exploring their capabilities and that you do through reading the script with them and then the session of improvisation continues for a considerable period of time. Even if you know an actor there is a need for him to re-invent himself and explore his caliber to be cast in a given role. No matter how great an actor is when he is put into a fresh situation of a fresh script and in an altogether new character, he faces stumbling blocks and there the director has to draw on his creative skill to help the actor cross them.

This process has to be done in a different way with each actor because each actor has his unique personality and in my thirty-five years of experience I have seen that there are no readymade methods of doing it. Many times even when you are working with an actor you have known well, you have to invent a different approach for different plays and characters. At times, I have also seen not only the interpretation changing with a different actor but the interpretation of the play changing with the change of cast.

Right now what comes to my mind is my production of Eugene Ionesco's *The Lesson*. The first time I produced this play with Jayshree –who was my classmate – as the maid, the character came about as a very genuine person who tries her best to prevent the tragedy to repeat itself by constantly warning the professor not to indulge in stabbing his pupil. But when I produced this play with Uttara Baokar as the maid, I realised that it is the maid who operates in the background and actually instigates the professor to re-enact the tragedy. This was my debut production after I passed out from NSD. I learnt a great lesson that with the change of cast a play can acquire a very different meaning. I think it happened because of the personalities of these two actresses which came to interplay with the characters and also because of their experiences in the field of acting. While Uttara was already a mature and seasoned actor, Jayshree was still a fresh person, groping in the field of acting. But both are extremely talented actresses in their own way; both of them are Sangeet Natak Akademi's awardees.

'Similarly, in the case of *Samrat – The Last War of Ashok*, initially it was Shyam Kumar in the role of Ashok. He made the character more archetypically heroic and larger-than-life—a common perception of Ashok in the Indian psyche. But when Mahendra Mewati did the same role, he made the character more human, who wept bitterly and suffered like any ordinary human being. Interestingly enough, both have their own validity and were convincing to the audience.

'Strangely enough I have seen totally fresh actors coming out with an excellent performance and bringing a character to life with all its shades and nuances. While a much more experienced and extremely gifted actor can always fall short of expectations. This was what happened in the case of my production of my *Chandrama Singh Urf Chamku*, which I did initially with the students of NSD. Vipin Sharma played the lead role—Chamku. Vipin did not have any worthwhile experience as an actor but he gave a memorable performance which people remember till date. I again did the play with the Repertory Company of NSD in which Raghuvir Yadav, a highly experienced and gifted actor, did the role of Chamku, but could not achieve the wonder of Vipin's performance. Yadav had seen Vipin's performance and he could not liberate himself from the memory of Vipin's portrayal. Probably, if he had not seen Vipin's performance, he would have approached the character differently and had come out with an equally mesmerising performance. The same thing happened with Om Puri when he performed in the role of the professor in the *The Lesson*. In the first instance, Naseer had acted in that role when I did it for my examination as the student director. The play was revived by the Repertory of NSD. Naseer was not available. Om Puri stepped into the role. He was extremely uncomfortable and felt he would not be able to achieve what Naseer has achieved in the role of professor. I had to coerce and cajole him and literally guided him into the process of delineation of the character. Eventually, he also came with a convincing performance. Naseer's portrayal was still better. I think it again happened because of the different temperament and personalities these two highly gifted actors had. Naseer is a thinking actor, his approach is more intellectual while most of the actors play through instinct and emotions. In this case, Naseer's approach suited the character better.

'I read *The Lesson* once again. The play operates on very many levels but it also offers the possibility of various interpretations, particularly a play like this, which is a poetic tragic comedy. This collective give-and-take only makes theatre a truly democratic art discipline. Director should always be flexible not only between actors but also between actors themselves.'

A contemporary director's main concern is the changes that are taking place in the art of acting. Having trained in a variety of acting styles at NSD under the guidance of E. Alkazi, his subsequent exposure was to classical and modern acting styles in Japan. This was followed by his work in relation to the Bheel tribals of Udaipur and his in-depth study of Gavari, the traditional Bheel theatre and interactions with tribal rituals and beliefs. With this background, Bharti has been constantly enriching his experience as a director, re-inventing himself, expanding the horizon of his art.

According to Bhanu, Indian theatre and art of acting are going through crisis. He comments: 'We are living in the worst phase of capitalism. In capitalism it is only the material wealth that matters. All progress is capital-centric and when you create capital there is nothing important then the market and the market forces are dominating human relations, freedom of expression and creativity[2].

'After industrialisation, the colonisation of Asia, Africa and Latin America began. After years of slavery the enslaved people liberated themselves inflicting ignoble defeat to capitalism.

'But neo-colonisation became the new face of capitalist exploitation. Now, new markets could be created and expanded through remote controls and mechanisation. In such eventuality what matters is the commodity which sells—either you produce or sell it or purchase or consume. In this kind of situation the first casualty is the human contact beyond the market situation without any kind of material give and take. So there is a conscious effort to destroy the social fabric and render a man insecure and lonely and therefore vulnerable to market forces. Neo-colonisation also very consciously acts against thoughts and creativity and also bulldozes the cultural diversification and variants. It creates robots which think alike, speak alike, eat alike and dress alike.

Corporate culture thrives in such ambience. It needs a flat surface without any contours.

'The crisis of theatre and acting is a reflection of the crisis of modern man and society which face a void; man's faith and belief in fellow human beings and social moorings are gradually eroding. In order to perform in theatre you have to believe in what is not real—what is imaginary; what is not material but metaphoric. When you lose faith and do not share beliefs with other persons and do not have any believe in yourself, then a very deep crisis of communication takes roots. The communication at a deeper level is sharing, a real communication takes place when you have to share something with other and when there is nothing to share then there is nothing to communicate or to express. Loneliness breeds a worst kind of spiritual desert in a man and in society and in this kind of spiritual desert no theatre is possible because theatre in its essence is a communal art and demands a very deep sense of sharing and togetherness to experience something which goes much beyond the everyday life experience. This explains the crisis of an actor in our times because in order to act we have to believe in something which does not correspond to your day-to-day reality, which takes you into uncharted territories, which demands from you and from an actor a very deep-rooted faith not only in his art but also in his fellow creators, including the audience.'

Talks with some of the actors and actresses who have performed under his direction reveal his style of working with his members of the cast as well as his approach to a play. The actors interviewed who has acted in his path-breaking productions provide an insight into his style of working with actors and gives contours of the way he realizes the concept of his production,

A 1995 pass-out of NSD, Mahendra Mewati worked with the NSD's Repertory from 1995-2000. Under the direction of Bhanu, he acted in *Aks-Tamasha* as Prince, the lead role. He has also acted in Bhanu's productions in a variety of roles. He delineated Ashok in *Samrat* and lawyer in *Hedda Gabler* as Teji Brar. He recounts his experience of working with Bhanu:

'I had already played the lead role in *Thank You Baba Lochan Das* under the direction of B.M. Shah. It was a tremendous success. Then we were asked to do *Aks-Tamasha* to be directed by Bhanuji. I was complacent. He interacted with us. He said he needed something different from what we had been doing. Apparently, not satisfied with the kind of acting we have been doing in a routine manner, he decided to take a theatre workshop for twenty-five days. As for the very complex role of Prince, he said he needed an actor who could portray a character which is a man and at the same time a woman. He explained the concept of *Ardhnareshwar*. He asked who is ready to play this role. There was silence and then I raised my hand.

'Rehearsals began on a serious note. One day I was late for rehearsals by ten minutes. He was angry and gave this role to Vijay Raaz. I was asked to join casuals. I was depressed. Then he decided to have double cast for this role.

'I watched him selecting masks minutely. He examined them one by one; not satisfied, he rejected ten masks and continued rejecting them until he was fully satisfied. He was a perfectionist in every aspect of theatrical art, music, costumes, sets, sound and lighting were critically supervised by him. He would leave nothing to chance. He is so demanding and knowledgeable that I felt scared by his presence.

'I found a great deal of difference between his approach and the approach of other directors. Some directors at the NSD's Repertory show us video clips of their previous productions of the same play or the presentation of the play by eminent

Directors and would ask us to follow the same acting style. Bhanuji never followed this kind of practice. Most of the directors accept of style of acting of previous directors, I had often question their style but I surrender to Bhanuji.

This does not mean that Bhanuji treats his actors as puppets. He projects a broad countours of the character to convey his vision and he leaves details to the ingenuity of the actor. At the same time he does not allow his actors to transgress framework he has visualized. He keeps on rehearsing until he discovers a dialectical unity between his vision and the vision of the actor.

'Portraying the Prince in *Aks-Tamasha* is a great portrayal of my life. The Prince is a woman as well as a man; he is a snake as well as a

Prince. When using symbols created by complex interplay of music, lighting and mask the Prince is cut into two pieces from head to torso, two antagonistic forces are separated – poisonous snake out to destroy humanity and an innocent and kind hearted youth. This kind of bold and rare experiment even Alkazi could not undertake. This entire experiment on the stage was unbelievable both for me and the audience.

'Similarly, playing the role of Ashok and the lawyer in Teji Brar was challenging. I listened carefully what Bhanuji wanted and watched me to portray these roles during rehersals, improvising the way I wanted to present. The good thing about Bhanuji's direction is that he allows his actors freedom to use their imagination.

'As far as *Samrat* is concerned I really lived it. On the opening night as soon as the dhow was over, I went to green room. Bhanuji followed me. He was furious and shouted. "This is not Samrat - the *Samrat* of my vision. I want a genuine Samrat." At night I received a call from him suggesting the ways I could improve my Samrat. The following evening he was very pleased with my portrayal and congratulated me. Presenting this play at Gawhauti, Agartala and Shillong had a different kind of excitement. The play was being presented in the midst of danger of flare up of violence. To counter this violence Samrat was preaching the great lesson of non-violence, the futility of bloodshed of innocent people. Here the artists were playing their social role to create a fearless society. These shows were witnessed by a paceked hall in rapt attention, establishing perfect rapport with the performers. The character of Ashok has reached a high point of a great historic character. It all thrilled me immensely what a joy it was to see an audience burst into thunderous applause, this is the magic of theatre, the magic created through the collaborative creativity of the director and his cast.

'When Teji Brar was presented at BNA, Luknow the audiences were overwhelmed with the illusion of reality created on the stage.

'I've also worked under his direction in Dario Fo's *We Won't Pay! We Won't Pay!*, a farce in which I play four characters- Hawaldar, Inspector, Tabootman and Longman - which required change of costume and different style of acting.

'When Bhanuji directs a play, he is never awed by great actors. For him Nasseer and a fresh actor are equal. He gives equal respect to all performers, using all his resources to fire their imagination to reach to the correct solution.

'Bhanuji is a versatile director, 'I don't hate him, I don't love him, I simply adore him.

"A 1993 pass out of NSD, Harvinder Kaur expressed her experiences working under the direction of Bhanu. She was with the NSD Repertory Company from 1993-'99. When Bhanu was doing *Aks-Tamasha* for the Repertory in 1996. He cast her in the role of Mayawati, the mother of the Prince. She described her experience.

'I was asked to read the script with focus on my character, visualizing the ambience in which the action is set, Bhanuji discussed with me the character, her social status and her deep anxiety for her son. He told me to internalise the character traits of Mayawati and her complex emotional world. Then there was intensive practice to strike the right gestures, postures. The director also wanted serious practice of intonation, pause, and expressions. Mayawati, the queen is always obsessed with the impending death of her son, the prince.

The director wanted to deliver the very line to express the inner dilemma of the Queen, her relation with the wife of her son who has sexual relations with a snake which is in fact not a snake but a part of the Prince himself. The production was a combination of realism and stylization. Bhanuji after working with actors vigorously, individually and collectively leave some space for actor's innovation. This gave me freedom to recreate my portrait of my character at once compelling and intricate. Bhanuji's process is long but he allows the actor to resolve conflict, using his or her imagination within the broad framework he had devised.

'I have worked under him in Teji Brar, playing the role of Priya and in another production I played the role of aunt. In all these performances I discovered in Bhanuji style a kind of Brechtian shade, allowing his actors to keep some distance between themselves and the character.

'In contrast, Satyadev Dubey's style of direction is highly calculated; the actor has to follow everything the director had conceived in detail.

Bhanu excels in guiding the actors in a stylized production. The use of masks and music score were simply great. *Aks-Tamasha* is a milestone. It should be revived under his direction to enable theatre practitioners and audience to watch a rare theatrical feat."

Rama, a Hindi professor and SRC Acting course pass-out had acted under the direction of Bhanu in a few plays. Her performance in three different characters in *Maha Mayi* was widely acclaimed. Here she narrates her experience.

'I played three women of different age and social background. I had to change costumes in a jiffy.

'Bhanuji was not interested in projecting these characters through external attributes. He wanted transformation through body language and speech patterns. The internal emotions should be reflected through action. To achieve this challenging creative task I went through vigorous training under Bhanuji. It was really a satisfying performance, delineating these different characters. The play had several shows in Delhi and the Prithvi theatre Mumbai where it evoked tremendous response from the audience.

'I have also acted in a few other productions under the direction of Bhanu. As an actress to work with him is highly rewarding and fulfilling'.

Trained as a Bharat Natyam dancer and a performer, Sindhu Bhagya Mishra was nineteen when Bhanu cast her in a leading female role in Sarveshwar Dayal Saxena's *Ab Garibi Hatao*. Since then their creative collaboration continues. In fact, her interaction with Bhanu has changed her perception about theatre and dance. Though at that time she had worked with two stage directors – Bansi Kaul and Anil Chaudhary. She decided to act only under Bhanu's direction. Over the years, she has collaborated in almost all productions of Bhanu in different capacity—lead actress, choreographer and costume designer. Sindhu talked about Bhanu's approach to performers with the knowledge of an insider:

'After visualising the concept of the production of a play Bhanuji explains his vision to his actors in an unaffected manner, free from theoretical jargon, easy to comprehend even by an average actor.

'Bhanuji cast me in the role of a common woman, representing exploited masses. I was then a second year student of Jawaharlal Nehru University and I was nineteen. Dancing was my passion but I also liked to act in a play. So the rehearsals began. After persistent efforts to follow the guidelines of the director, I was unable to come up to his expectations. In fact, Bhanuji never compromises with his art and his expectations from his actors are very high.

'He would tell me the class characteristics of my character. One day he shouted at me, "Don't float on the stage, don't make your gestures and postures delicate and lyrical. This is not dance". So I had to start to unlearn what I had acquired with so much rigorous training of a dancer.

'There was a rape scene. My character was being raped by a member of the ruling class. After rehearsing the scene for several days, Bhanuji was totally dissatisfied. At one such rehearsal I was suddenly taken aback when Bhanuji slapped me hard, not once but several times. I started bitterly weeping. I told myself that I did not do anything to deserve this kind of beating. He was standing near me and said, "Now you know what molestation means."[3] His emphasis was psychological and emotional revelation of the intensity of pain and humiliation. My problem became all the more difficult because the rapist was represented by a puppet. The persistence of mine and the director finally yielded excellent results [*sic*]. The Press and the audience were all praise for the production as a brilliant experimental piece of theatrical art. I was also praised as the highly imaginative actress who had portrayed a challenging role in a seeming effortless manner with intensity.

'With this performance I realised the power of theatre, I decided to work for the theatre and that too under the direction of Bhanuji only.

'Over the years, acting under his direction has unique experience, sweet-bitter, agonised and ecstatic. Perhaps this kind of dialectic experience is the soul of artistic creativity.

'In the course of rehearsal of *Naachni*, a one-woman performance with one and a half hours duration I had to face the ebb and flow of emotions. This marginalised, socially outcaste and sexually exploited woman is an artist *par excellence*. She is flooded with memories. She is denied the natural right to become a mother by a heartless society which considers a woman as a mere commodity. Kiran Sehgal was invited to do the choreography.

'After rehearsals we all came to a restaurant for lunch. We were tired. Kiran was all praise for my work. Bhanuji was silent and then he suddenly said with anxiety writ large on his face, "Sindhu, this is not coming out well, it's not working," I was shocked. Actually I wanted to hear praise for my work from his mouth, the kind of praise Kiran was showering on me. I composed myself and asked politely, "which portion is not coming to the fore?". Kiran expressed her displeasure at Bhanuji's comments. Breaking the silence Bhanuji said, "The character is as docile as a mouse, it is also as fierce as a tigress. She lives many lives with multiple emotional layers."

'Bhanuji is always in quest of excellence and it is very, very difficult to reach his level and it has been my persistent and conscious efforts to match his standards. With each new role I have to struggle hard and undergo tedious creative journey to achieve excellence.

'I was also associated with him in the process of writing of *Naachni*. Bhanuji would repeatedly say, "Don't sentimentalise the character of *Naachni*. If you draw yourself in tears you will not be able to do justice with the character. She is a far greater woman, deeper, brave and creative. She is not a stupid middle-class woman.

'Impressed with my performance in *Ab Garibi Hatao*, he cast me in his ambitious project of staging *Katha Kahi Ek Jale Ped Ne* but not in the lead role. I was depressed. He was looking for an established actress and holding negotiations with Anita and Mona Chawla. But I was rehearsing the main role of Monkey Queen on my own and would come straight from JNU to the rehearsal venue and would rehearse in the absence of the director and fellow actors. One day Bhanuji came earlier, He was watching me from a distance. I was oblivious of his presence. Finally, he selected me for this role, though I had to work very hard to know about the character to portray and interpret it and worked on the voice pattern because all the characters in the play were monkeys. I got excellent reviews for my performance.

'Playing the role of Teji Brar (*Hedda Gabler*) was full of challenges. Some call it character study, for some she is cold and repulsive. I was confused. In the course of rehearsals, Finally, she emerged before me as a positive person and endowed with the strength of character.'

'A member of NSD faculty, Lokendra Trivedi had worked under the direction of Bhanu as his actor and was associate director in *Yum Gatha* which was directed by Bhanu. Lokendra acted in *The Elephant* under the direction of Bhanu. He talked about his interaction with Bhanu as his actor in *Yum Gatha* and Bernard Shaw's *Pygmalion*. Lokendra expressed his opinion about Bhanu in the following lines:

'He is a modern director but he has vast resources drawn from traditional, folk and tribal arts in terms of music, design, dance, costumes and rituals. With a view to make explicit the political philosophy of *Yum Gatha* as a conflict between Aryans and non-Aryans, he took us to South India in tribal belts. He had done in-depth study of history, sociology and anthropology to portray the antagonistic forces at constant war. On the one hand there were non-Aryans, asserting their cultural identity and on the other there were gods headed by Indra who were determined to enslave non-Aryans with brute force. Different kind of dialogue delivery was devised for different classes. Vedic chanting with the help of Sanskrit language was formed part of the dialogue for Indra and the gods. I was playing the role of Vibhavak.

'He is a director who wants complete devotion to work from his cast, stimulates their curiosities to know all aspects of theme and theatrical technique. he envisages the visual and aural aspects of a production to convey the essence of the play in an intricate manner.

'He studied context seriously and discovers its form out of its content. There is a dialectical unity in his production of the form and content. What is most noteworthy is that his every production has a new presentational style and theatre language. I was associated in his three productions all were different in technique. He never repeats himself.

'In *Yum Gatha* we used to rehearse till the wee hours and then we would sleep there at the rehearsal space in the open, the female artists were sent home in taxis. For we actors it was a rare event and a new discovery.

'*Yum Gatha* was an epic production with nearly seventy performers and a whole lot of technicians and stage hands. Bhanuji has a special art to bring out the very best from an actor. I have seen this in his productions like *Aazar Ka Khwab* (*Pygmalion*) in 1988. G.P. Namdev as Aazar and Himani Shivpuri as Amrudwali (Hajjo) reached the peak of their acting career. It is said that they cannot sustain that excellence for long.'

Rooted in tradition, Bhanu never repeats; he is an innovator and keeps reinventing. As a stage director he had interacted with professionally trained actors, amateurs and tribal performers. Recounting his experience of working with different category of actors, he says:

'Professionally trained actors contribute to the production. You don't have to teach them the basics of acting. You are at least confident that they will attain certain level and are dependable. But it has rarely happened that the professional and trained actors have given me a surprise. I can remember very few such instances. Immediately what comes to my mind are the performances of Surekha Sikri, Jyoti Deshpandey in my production of *Ras-Gandharva* which I did for NSD repertory back in 1974. I cajoled them into accepting male roles and both performed superbly. They played roles of convicts in a jail; their costumes were loose knee-long kurta and pyjamas. People in the audience could hardly recognise them as fully grown up female actresses, they took them for vagabonds, indulging in antics, smoking bidies and mouthing four-letter words. Though fully convinced of their talents, I had myself not imagined the kind of great performance they gave. But I mostly found that trained actors tend to develop certain mannerisms and it's very difficult to get the truth out of his or her performance. I have also experienced that barring a few like Uttara Baokar, Surekha Sikri, Naseer and occasionally Manohar Singh, most of our trained actors are only semi-professionals, the training they get in the drama schools is not proper. We have not yet evolved the right kind of training methodology for our urban actor in our theatre teaching institutions, NSD included. The biggest casualty is the speech. Till date, whatever our actors have learnt in our theatre institutions is through performance and experience.

'I found working with amateur actors more fruitful. You can mould them into a character easily and extract a totally truthful performance. It happened many times. For instance my production of *Tambe ke Kide* which had such a freshness about it that it struck a deep cord with the audience. The same thing I can say about Sindhu Bhagya Mishra's performances in *Ab Garibi Hatao* and *Katha kahi Jale Ped Ne*. She had achieved a level of performance, especially in *Katha Kahi* which no other actress had surpassed. She played the role of a monkey queen in an environmental setting, climbing up the ladder, performing on high-rise small platforms stuck between trees.

The kind of vitality, elegance she brought to her performance was absolutely mesmerising. I remember the children (all girls) of Mayo College in Ajmer performing in an adaptation of Prem Chand's novel *Godan*. The truthfulness that these young girls could bring to their performances was absolutely fascinating but breaking the ice with those amateur actors is the most crucial aspect of a director's job. These can never be a single, definite approach. Time is limited; there is little scope to train them. So you have to innovate your approach with each individual, which not only calls on your resources but at times is also emotionally exhausting for you and the person involved. I admit that at times I have even been cruel with some of the amateur actors.'

Bhanu's experience of working with Bheel tribals have already been described in the chapters on productions inspired by Gavari.

Endnotes:

1. *The Profession of the Stage Director* by Georgi Tovstonogov.
2. About 150 years ago, Karl Marx wrote: "It (economy) transforms fidelity into infidelity, love into hate, hate into love, virtue into vice, vice into virtue, servant into master, idiocy into intelligence and intelligence into idiocy. ... He who can buy bravery is brave though he be a coward."
3. Rape is a crime of violence. Most rapists have the precise purpose of humiliating and harming the victim. The rapist finds sexual pleasure in the victim's pain and fear. The victim's sexual compliance may even increase the intensity of the rapist's aggression. —*Bad Men Do What Good Men Dream* by Robert I. Simon, M.D

A conversation with Bhanu

The artist is the sensitive recipient of all that (which) affects his country and his class: he is its ear, eye and heart; he is the voice of his time. He is duty bound to know as much as he can, and the better he knows the past, the better he will understand the present, and the more deeply and keenly will he realise the universal revolutionaries of our time and the scope of the tasks confronting it.

—Maxim Gorky

Art not only reproduces life but explains it: its production very often "has the purpose of pronouncing judgment on the phenomenon of life."

Chernyshevsky (as quoted by
G. Plekhanov in *Art and Social Life*)

Q: Against a brief background of the history of Indian theatre, what is the present scenario of contemporary theatre?

A: For historical reasons theatre in India disintegrated and disappeared from the mainstream in the medieval times. Whatever remained of theatre remained in rural India or manifested in what you may call 'folk' tradition and in some temples located deep down in South India. Theatre made a comeback with the consolidation of colonial rule in India.

Obviously, this theatre was totally influenced by the British and through them by western tradition. The long colonial rule also created a wide gulf within the agricultural population in the vast rural landscape of the country and the newly emerging Anglicised middle class in the urban areas. It was this middle class which started theatre practice first as an amateurish activity confined to the drawing rooms of aristocrats but soon enough the educated middle class intelligentsia realised the potential of the theatre as a tool for cultural renaissance in the country. Theatre in the native languages, particularly in Bengal and Maharashtra came into being, which addressed the socio-cultural issues of the times. Some major talents like Girish Ghosh and others emerged and an authentic theatre found root in the urban middle class society of the nineteenth society. At the same time, some Parsi entrepreneurs in the newly emerging commercial centre – Bombay – realised the commercial potential and formed large theatre companies to perform in the vast Hindi belt and also in the emerging metropolises like Calcutta, Bombay and Delhi for a wider viewership and commercial success. These companies drew heavily from the popular musical traditions, which have been kept alive by the *tawaifs* (courtesans) of *kothas* (community living quarters of courtesans) and popular agrarian theatre traditions like Nautanki and Tamasha. But these companies also borrowed not only the plots – mostly from Shakespeare – but also the presentational styles of the commercial musicals of Europe's painted sceneries and the revolving stage. This unique mix of popular folk tradition and European commercial theatre came to be known as Parsi theatre which instantly became popular with the urban and semi-urban aristocracy and the middle classes. But with the advent of cinema the Parsi theatre died its natural death and again a vacuum was created in theatre.

Post-independence era gave birth to a theatre which saw the emergence of theatre professionals like Ebrahim Alkazi, Habib Tanvir and Utpal Dutt who were properly trained in the schools of Britain. A crop of modern playwrights like Mohan Rakesh, Badal Sircar, Girish Karnad and Vijay Tendulkar started writing plays, reflecting the problems of the urban middle class society which was suffering acutely from the disillusionment of the post-Nehruvian era and ever increasing unemployment and economic deprivation.

I have gone into this lengthy background so that we can understand the situation where a need was felt to look beyond the confines of the middle class strait-jacketing of theatre (as a genre) and its colonial hangover. By now there was a sizeable number of professionally trained theatre workers within the country wishing to create a theatre which would connect them to the new experiences of democratic polity of their own times. There was a need to take a fresh look at the past rural culture and its vitality.... It was this contemplation which led some of us to connect closely with the eastern theatre traditions in general and our folk traditions in particular.

But unfortunately I find that barring a handful of my contemporaries most have succumbed to the stylistic exotica of these traditions rather than creating a meaningful synthesis of the rural and the urban sensibilities to give vent to the anguish and express the hopes of our people in the contemporary scenario.

I feel the entire movement has been derailed into a meaningless cliché of creating indigenous theatre or connecting to the roots or reviving a tradition for its own sake. … what is important is to bridge the gap between the rural and the urban and create a theatre to overcome the colonial past and connect to the aspirations of the people of this young democracy with ancient cultural memories. It is a stupendous task and it is about time that we wake up to this socio-cultural need of our people.

Q: Why was the movement derailed?
A: I think we Indians are experts in creating confusion and derailing things. It has happened all through history—from Buddha right down to Gandhi. Things have been emptied of their contents and the forms have been retained. It is somewhat like swallowing the contents of an egg and keeping the cell intact. The same was true about Indian theatre; what was vital and important was shrouded with confusion. This led to the derailment of a movement.

Q: These days you have been directing medleys of folk dances and songs like *Bharat Utsav, Lok Tarang for Pravasi Bharatis*. How you will define this kind of work—a fusion, a spectacle or what?

A: Gandhiji had said India lives in its villages. Even today we talk of two Indias—the India living in the cities and India in its villages. I have already discussed this gulf which exists not only in the realm of economics but also in all aspects of socio-cultural life. After Independence there have been half-hearted efforts to reduce this gulf but after the globalisation of the economy and strengthening of the market forces in India this gulf has widened to an alarming extent. It manifests itself in the suicides of the farmers, agitations in Singur and Nandigram, the Naxalite and other separatist movements. The urban elite in the country displays complete disdain for the people and their socio-cultural plight in the rural areas. This apathy and insensitivity reflects at all levels and spheres. Whatever little scope we create for this vast rural population of the country is created under compulsion—under the garb of charity towards our poor cousins. This apathy is equally widespread in the field of culture. Forget the folk and rural cultures in the present scenario. Is there any scope for any kind of serious artistic or cultural activities?

Please forgive me for this digression but it is important to have the context right. As I was telling you that there are half-hearted and cosmetic efforts at connecting to the culture at the grassroots and the tendency to commercially exploit this vast talent from the rural India in the name of fusion. This tendency is most manifested in the field of music where commercial compositions have exploited the talent of folk singers and musicians in the name of fusion. I cannot change this scenario all by myself but whenever given an opportunity I have tried to bring forth the living force of folk culture with all its vitality into a synthesised whole. I have attempted this synthesis without disturbing the ethos and the substance of the folk forms and by exploring their innate vigour which manifests itself in the robust mind and body of rural India.... I am glad for the little I did in this sphere which attracted a serious notice and the people beyond rural confines have realised this strength and relevance of this grass root culture.

Q: Under the Sangeet Natak Akademi scheme to provide financial assistance to talented young directors to assimilate traditional folk and tribal theatre elements into modern Indian theatre you have created experimental theatrical works remarkable for ingenuity, new ideas and universal relevance. You are still working with the Bheel tribals of Udaipur, Rajasthan. Gradually, this scheme has degenerated into the revival of ritualistic folk forms as a mere decorative piece. What is your opinion on such theatrical experiments?

A: At the onset I want to clarify that my interaction with Bheel ritual Gavari has nothing to do with finding an Indian identity of theatre. Theatre being a social art and not an individualistic expression has to have localised roots. It cannot exist in a vacuum. When I entered theatre in the early '70s I encountered a theatre which was middle class and highly urbanised. Mohan Rakesh, Vijay Tendulkar, Badal Sircar and Girish Karnad were the playwrights who had emerged as the torchbearers of modern Indian theatre but … the sensibilities of those plays did not satisfy me. I somehow found this theatre … largely rootless. Therefore from the very beginning I tried to look beyond these playwrights and their sensibilities.

It was the search which took me to Mani Madhukar's *Ras-Gandharva* which was my first production after passing out from the NSD in 1973. *Ras-Gandharva,* though not a very significant play and lacking in the craft very badly, somehow liberated itself from that urban middle class sensibility of Rakesh and Tendulkar. After *Ras-Gandharva* I discovered Bhuwaneshwar Prasad in his *Tambe Ke Kide* which I produced in Luknow in 1974. I discovered a playwright who had developed an indigenous idiom of Hindi theatre back in the 1940s. He had evolved a Theatre of the Absurd, which was totally free of western influence and yet modern and authentically rooted in the experience of the society it talked about. Mind you he wrote *Tambe Ke Kide* before Ionesco or Beckett came on the scene and after that I discovered Dharamvir Bharati's *Andha Yug* … a contemporary classic. Since then I have produced the play three or four times including a show in Nepal which evoked a tremendous response among theatre goers as well as with the press.

A Nepali newspaper wrote an editorial referring to its relevance to a society in quest of human values devastated by meaningless war. The play still captivates me … it was very natural for me to look for a theatrical idiom which would not be straitjacketed in urban sensibilities influenced by western Modernist world view. I took a fellowship from the Sangeet Natak Akademi and went to study the folk theatre in Rajasthan, particularly Khayal as practised by Ugam Raj. As the same time I went with Habib Tanvir to Chhattisgarh to attend his workshop on Nacha performers. I was also greatly inspired by Habib's *Agra Bazaar*. And then I went to Japan to study Noh and Kabuki. In Japan, apart from Noh and Kabuki what inspired me most was Bunraku which is Japan's puppet theatre. This experience further convinced me to look beyond western realism and rediscover the tradition of Indian theatre kept alive in the folk theatres practised throughout the country. After I returned from Japan I experimented with Sarveshwar Dayal Saxena's *Ab Garibi Hatao*. After that came *Katha Kahi Ek Jale Ped Ne* which was based on an allegorical short story by Kijima Hajima, which I chanced upon in Japan. I used a vast open-air space including high tree trunks and, bamboo ladders.

I narrated this long background just to show that since the very beginning I was highly dissatisfied with the mainstream theatre of the '70s and the '80s and was constantly striving to break free and find an idiom which would connect me to the socio-cultural reality.

It is in the above light that my interaction with Gavari should be understood. I wanted to experience Bheel rituals from close quarters and I also wanted to study a community still rooted in shared beliefs and communal consciousness which the urban society has lost long since. My interaction with them was conscious and of an analytical kind. I did not pretend to be an insider nor did I try to imitate or extract a slice of their culture and package it for the consumption of the urban elite, always eager to decorate their drawing rooms with folk or rural artefacts chosen randomly without any context and connection. This conscious and analytical approach gave me a profound insight into the very essence of theatre ... what gives theatre the magic to operate on so many layers of the conscious and the subconscious.

My production of *Pashu Gayatri, Kaal Katha* and *Amar Beej* are experiments towards discovering that authentic and magical theatrical experience.

Q: During Emergency did you face problems as a director to stage plays? What is your opinion about freedom of the artist?
A: I didn't face much problem, thanks to the idiotic censor machinery operating at the time. I remember I was doing Mohit Chattopadhyay's political play *Guinea Pig* which talks about the exploitative character of the state machinery no matter in which garb, whether feudal or democratic. The head of the institution for which I was to produce this play came to me and told me that Emergency had been proclaimed and we would have to send the script for censor. 'I don't think, they will allow us to stage it,' said the head of the institution.

To everybody's surprise the play was cleared by the censoring authorities. Finally, the show was on. The District Commissioner who was present in the audience, was uncomfortable but couldn't have said anything because the script was duly certified. But certainly theatre has faced worst kinds of censorship all over the world.

The power and potential of theatre is very well known to all political establishments of all hues and ideologies and establishments at one point or the other have tried to silence theatre. All arts by way of their very nature are anti-status quo and therefore anti-establishment. It cannot remain immune to the realities of life that neo-colonisation has created – a world without distinction between local identities – in order to provide a level playing field to the market forces.

A faceless, characterless, mindless world has been attempted but we already see a resistance to these forces, emerging all over in terms of environment, cultural and ethnic protests. Theatre being a social and human activity cannot remain divorced to the most important social and political questions of our times. It has to reflect all these concerns. Other art forms like music and painting are trying to find a market. Theatre cannot be canned and marketed. It is an organic art form, nurtured by its own environment.

There is a serious threat to our artists and writers. The FIR (First Information Report) was registered against me on flimsy grounds for hurting the religious sentiments of the majority community. We are passing through a phase where there is a growing intolerance towards artistic expression like never before and we have no option but to work in this kind of stultifying environment. It is time for the theatre community to fight unitedly for the preservation of freedom of expression. The ever-shrinking democratic space and the right to dissent have to be protected. In our own ways we have to continue the tradition of producing anti-establishment works of art even at the risk of antagonising the state … (the) voice dissent is our fundamental duty.

Q: What do you think about theatre criticism in India?
A: All along the creative people from all disciplines have suffered from critics and criticism. Theatre is no exception. Theatre, particularly in India is the worst suffer. It is ironical that theatre needs (immediate) criticism because it only survives in the present. A book can be read even after 200 years … but theatre cannot wait for posterity to take cognizance. But unfortunately in India we do not have informed critics and serious criticism is yet to be found. I am not stating it for the first time. I have been stating it all through my 'brief' career of theatre practice of nearly four decades.

Q. You have done two contemporary classics—*AndhaYug* and *Tughlaq* recently. Both these plays were staged in the open air against the backdrop of the historical ruins of Ferozshah Kotla on a scale unprecedented in the history of contemporary Indian theatre both in terms of production values, exploration of new expressive dimensions of the theatrical art. Would you like to continue with this programme, which has taken the shape of an annual event? How do you describe these productions as milestones in the history contemporary Indian theatre movement?
A. After the 1960s and 1970s theatre was relegated to the periphery. There were few attempts to rejuvenate interest in the theatre. Nothing significant was achieved. The Sangeet Natak Akademi held a retrospective in 1989, of plays which were produced in the 1960s and 1970s. The retrospective turned out to be a total failure. The productions revived for this festival have lost their vitality and relevance. After that a big opportunity was created for theatre in terms of an annual theatre festival organised under the auspices of the National School of Drama known as Bharat Rang Mahotsav. But it failed to gain momentum

because it lacks clarity of vision and has no objective system for the proper selection of plays.

I am happy that the plays you have mentioned invited widespread audience response and theatre reclaimed its place. That happened because as you have rightly said, *Andha Yug* and *Tughlaq* are modern Indian classics, which are more relevant today then they had been when they were written in the 1950s. They were not produced as an academic exercise but there was a conscious effort to gain fresh insight into both these plays and make them be in tune with contemporary times.

As far as continuing this experiment is concerned it will entirely depend on the Delhi government because without government support such productions are an impossibility. I will be happy if all the state governments take a cue from this experiment and work towards setting up professional theatre repertory in every region of the country. At least these productions have proved that given the resources, theatre can occupy a significant place in our society and it has not lost any of its relevance and magic.

Q. You have not done any Sanskrit classical play? Do you feel these plays and *Natyashastra* have lost contemporary relevance?
A. I have produced *Mrichchhakatikam* in Hindi translation in Jaipur in 1976. I think *Shakuntlam. Mrichchhakatikam, Urbhangam, Karnabhaam* make very relevant theatre for the future. They are great works of playwriting by all standards. But Sanskrit plays need exploration both in terms of staging and interpretation like all classics.

As far as *Natyashastra* is concerned it is the oldest treatise on theatre in the world and full of wonderful insights. It has a great educational value but following it literally creates problems.

Q. Now there is hardly any talk about going back to the roots to evolve an ingenious theatre idiom with the initiative of Sangeet Natak Akademi and the involvement of young theatre workers who were engaged in artistic cross-fertilisation—assimilating the heritage of the past to create a contemporary Indian theatre idiom. You were a bright star of this movement. Do you feel this movement has lost its relevance?

A. No, it is not that the movement has got itself embodied into contemporary theatre. Today our theatre has an identity of its own, independent of western shadow, which lingered till the seventies.

Q. You are a playwright also and writing plays is a creative act performed in a solitary state. These days there is a trend to evolve a script through a collaboration of actors and directors. Do you feel in future playwrights will have an increasingly marginal role to play?
A. A playwright plays a vital role and that is how it should be. A good play transcends its time and space and communicates different meanings in different times and milieu. How poor we would be if there were no Shakespeare, Moliere, Ibsen, Chekhov, Kalidas, Hasa, Sudrak etc. We still look towards them in the lean times for inspiration and hope.

Q. As a youth you were influenced by Marxism-Leninism. Where do we stand today? Is there political theatre in India?
A. All theatre is political because it is community activity. I was influenced by Marxism in my formative years and still hold true to the basic intent of Marxist philosophy. But I have realised over a period of time that man is not governed and should not be governed by the capital alone.

Man is not an economic animal. Economy plays a vital role in society but it is not the answer to all human needs. I think the human civilisation globally is at the crossroads where philosophies and ideologies have failed us in one way or the other and time has arrived where humanity is looking forward to a major break-through. My latest play *Tamasha Na Hua* raises this issue in a pertinent manner.

Q. What future do you visualise for theatre in the twenty-first century?
A. Theatre is an organic art form nurtured by its own environment. In this scenario I see a great future for theatre in the twenty-first century. People will throng to watch theatre in an unprecedented manner. We will be witness to a vibrant theatre culture which has never been witnessed in the past. I believe in the future of humanity and therefore I believe in the future of theatre.

Acknowledgements

I express my gratitude to the Ministry of Culture, Government of India, for awarding me a senior fellowship in the field of theatre, which enabled me to pursue the study of Bhanu Bharti's theatre.

Bhanu is a busy artist who frequently travels to different Indian cities and abroad. I am indeed thankful to him for allowing me to spend many evenings with him to discuss his work and his creative process. At times the discussions would continue till late night, often the focus shifting to wider issues about Indian culture and arts. It was indeed an enriching experience. He also allowed me to watch his rehearsals and interact with his actors. It is through his good offices, that I was able to stay for sometime at Udaipur and meet the Bheel performers.

Thanks to Bhagwan Lal Kachhawa, consultant on folk/tribal art and culture of Rajasthan for accompanying me to the villages of Bheels to watch Gavari for a full day, explaining to me the theme of the narrative and the meaning of the music with its distinctive style of rendition.

I am much obliged to Mr S. Thyagarajan, Chief Photographer, The National School of Drama for his painstaking efforts to make available photographs of some of Bhanu's old productions.

I am thankful to Ziya Us Salam, an aesthete and deputy editor of *The Hindu* for his support and encouragement. Many thanks to Dr Chandrasekhar Kambar, a great contemporary Indian playwright, for his inspiring Foreword to this book.

Special thanks to Niyogi Books and Mr Bikash D. Niyogi for publishing this book. Mr Niyogi's keen interest in the promotion of art and culture helped this book to see the light of day.

—Diwan Singh Bajeli